Carolyn

LADYCAKE FARM

LADYCAKE FARM

By Mabel Leigh Hunt

Illustrated by Clotilde Embree Funk

J. B. LIPPINCOTT COMPANY

PHILADELPHIA & NEW YORK

COPYRIGHT, 1952, BY MABEL LEIGH HUNT
PRINTED IN THE UNITED STATES OF AMERICA
FOURTH IMPRESSION

Library of Congress Catalogue Card Number 52–5107

91ℓ

Contents

CHAPTER ONE

Big Moment

Little Joe was eleven. He was old enough, therefore, to have discovered that sometimes the most amazing things do really happen. The days would be jog-trotting along, one after another, in the same old way, when, smacko!—one of them would become a Big Moment, so big as might fairly take a boy off his feet.

It was a big moment for Little Joe when Poppy told him they were going to move to the country. Of course Little Joe had known, ever since he had known anything, that Poppy's dearest wish was to own a farm. For the past two winters, Poppy had been going by bus to night school in Rozella, where there was a big agricultural college. Poppy not only had text books on soils, and reclaiming land, and farm management, but he had a stock of leaflets containing working rules for the planting and tending of crops, and for the raising of pigs and chickens. *How to Make a Living on the Small Farm*—Poppy had paid a dollar for that book. It was his favorite, and he knew it almost by heart. Little Joe did, too.

LADYCAKE FARM

To buy a small farm, Poppy had been saving part of the weekly wages he made by working at the lumber mill nearby. Poppy had done without a car. Mommy did her cooking on a wood stove. Shavings and scraps from the lumber mill helped out on fuel. Did Mommy even glance at the glittering enameled gas stoves in the windows of the Hoytville Hardware Company? Never! Did Poppy and Mommy believe they could not live if they did not possess a television set? They did not! Hadn't Little Joe and India Rose and Pearlie May done without many small things, and quite cheerfully, so that some day Poppy could buy a farm?

But it had been a dream farm, a beautiful thing which might possibly take shape after a long, long time. So that when Little Joe heard Poppy actually say, "Guess we're moving to our farm around the first of April," the boy was so astonished that for a wink of time he lost his breath.

But presently he began to giggle. "I'm sure a cat-fish outa water and puffin' on the bank," he sputtered. He couldn't stop giggling. Seemed as if the Big Moment had not only smacked him down, but was tickling him in the ribs.

Pearlie May, who was seven and the youngest, was astonished, also, but not as astonished as Little Joe. Pearlie May was used to listening to the weekly story hour at the Hoytville Public Library. The librarian told once-upon-a-time wonder stories with such big eyes and such a round *O* of a mouth that Pearlie May believed every word she said. Pearlie May had always known that moving to the country would be just another wonder story come true.

Nine-year-old India Rose was the least surprised of the three. India Rose believed that her poppy could work miracles, give him time and half a chance. "If Poppy has bought a farm," reasoned India Rose, "and is going to take us there—well, it was sure to happen to kids with a poppy like Poppy!"

But when the children heard *HOW* the moving was to be done—glory to goodness!—they just couldn't get it through their heads! That Saturday evening the very last of March they moseyed around in the yard, trying to figure it out. Pearlie May leaned over so far that her hair-ribbons brushed the earth, and peered under the five-room cottage which was their home in Hoytville.

"This house hasn't got legs," she mused. "So however can it walk away out to the country? Little Joe, maybe Poppy's only funnin'."

"Maybe Poppy could be playing an April Fool's joke on us, telling us the house is going to the farm, same as us," suggested India Rose. "No! Our poppy wouldn't do that."

"How many times I got to tell you that Poppy and Mommy say it's the hones' truth an' hope-to-die?"

scolded Little Joe. However, he also leaned over and looked through the wooden slats of the foundation.

"I'll be scared," faltered India Rose. "When this house starts moving, maybe everything will go to smash." India Rose's eyes were enormous in her dark little face. Joe and Pearlie May stared back at her, solemnly.

Mommy came to the door. "All for nothing do you give yourselves goosebumps of scare," she said, smiling. "Creep in, now, and go to bed, peaceable, or no one will have the strength tomorrow to pack and tether, and do the baking, and get everything shipshape for the big moving, come Monday."

There! Mommy had said it again—*the big moving,* come Monday! Her eyes were as bright with excitement as those of her children, Pearlie May, India Rose, and Little Joe. Once more she explained it all.

"How come, I tell you, Chicks. Mr. Tom Sargent, who owns the lumber mill, says to your poppy, 'Big Joe Freed, I aim to largen the mill. I need more ground, so I'd like to buy your home lot. How much you want, Big Joe, for your lot?'

" 'With my house thrown in, Mister Tom?' asked your poppy.

" 'I'm not int'rested in the house,' says Mister Tom.

BIG MOMENT

" 'Then give me time to dicker for the forty-acre farm I've had my wishing eye on,' says your poppy. 'At last it's for sale. If I get it, I'll take my house along.'

"So your poppy and Mister Tom make a fair bargain, an' settle up, and your poppy pays down on the forty acres he's had his wishing eye on. But first, Mister Tom drives out to the country and talks nice about your poppy to the farmers roun' about. Mister Tom says to them; 'Big Joe Freed is a friend of mine. He's a hard-working, upright colored man. He will make a good little farm out of those forty acres. And if you ever want to swap work with him, you will find him plenty strong and plenty willing. Now, folks,' says Mister Tom to the farmers, 'will you let Big Joe Freed come into this section 'thout making any trouble for him, jus' because his skin is brown?'

"The farmers scratch their heads and think. And then they answer, 'Long as he keeps his weeds down, and his stock penned up, and minds his business and don't raise any ruckus, let Big Joe Freed farm his forty acres in peace.' All but one farmer answered the same. All but one," said Mommy. "So we're moving. Your poppy and your mommy kept the news snug from you. We didn't want it to get you all fevered up, an' maybe pinch your school work. The farm's about five miles out of Hoytville. I've

13

not seen it myself," finished Mommy, glowing. "But we can trust your poppy that it's worth moving to."

"I'll say it is!" came a shout from the entry. Big Joe himself strode into the room. He swept Mommy and his children into a quick, wrap-around hug. "Once we've got it on the mend, that farm will be a dandy!" he cried. "I've had a new cellar dug out and cemented. I've had new foundations laid out of the rock base the old farmhouse stood on before it was burned two years ago, and its folks left the place for good. And let me tell you something! There's a tree in our front yard, an' the likes of it you never saw! It's so tall the stars hang in its branches at night. When we set our little house on the new foundations waiting under that tree, it won't look bad, not half bad." Poppy grinned from ear to ear. Little Joe, India Rose and Pearlie May grinned, too. They knew Poppy was talking small about a thing of which he was vasty proud.

"What kind of a tree is it, Poppy?" asked Little Joe.

"Maple tree," answered Poppy. "Friendliest kind."

" 'Friendliest kind,' " echoed Mommy, laughing out as happily as her children.

"Shall we lazy in the shade of that tree and rest ourselves?" asked Little Joe.

"When we're tired from our plowin' and plantin' and hoein', we'll lazy ourselves under that tree. Noble big and tall—that tree."

"How noble big?" begged Pearlie May.

"It spreads from here to yon." Poppy held out his arms, wide.

"How noble tall, Poppy?" coaxed India Rose.

"I told you, so noble tall the stars hang in its branches."

"Ooo-ooooh!" breathed India Rose and Pearlie May.

"I'm thinking our tree is going to be greatly dear to us," Mommy said.

"It sure will," promised Poppy. "And we'll have us a corn field," he went on, "and a pasture of clover and rye. We'll have us a garden patch, and garden sass. We'll have laying hens. I've already dickered for a young sow. Before you know it, she'll have a lot of curly-tailed piglets. We'll have a cow."

There was breathless silence in the cottage, while the children's minds stretched enough to take in the wonders of ownership—a pig and hens and a cow, garden sass and a corn field.

"But, Poppy!" cried Little Joe, at last. "I can't get it through my head. However we going to tote this house five miles and set it under that noble big tree?"

"Who said *we* going to tote, Son?" Poppy's laughter rolled out, rich and slow as molasses gurgling from a jug. "Why, you and Mommy and Indy Rose and Pearlie May going to do nothing but sit inside, easy, an' twiddle your thumbs, while the house rolls along as smooth as butter. Ol' Temple the mover, with his mules and his rollers, ropes and pulleys— he's going to drag us. We've got the say-so from the county to move our house over the roads."

"Where will you be, Poppy, while we roll along as smoove as butter?" asked Pearlie May.

"Once I know you're rolling, I'll go to work, same as every day. This is my last week at the mill until next winter. *Jubilee!*" shouted Poppy. "I can hardly wait to see my house standing under that big tree, and Mommy and my children snug as four buttons in a row of buttonholes."

Little Joe and India Rose and Pearlie May climbed into their beds, full of laughter at such an enchanting picture. They dreamed of the coming journey, the ol' mules high-tailing swiftly down the road, pulling the house. Smooth as butter it would roll, smooth as golden farm butter!

CHAPTER TWO

The Moving

The next day was Sunday. There was work to do before the big moving tomorrow. As the Freeds worked, they sang hymns to keep the Sabbath. When they came to the "hallelujahs," didn't they almost split their throats with joy? Sometimes they asked Pearlie May to sing, all by herself. Pearlie May could sing like a bird in a tree.

Mommy boiled a ham and a mess of hominy. She baked beans and ginger cakes. There must be plenty to eat while the mules were dragging the house to the country, and the cooking fire was outened. After Sunday dinner, Mommy packed her best dishes. She got out enough everyday ones to do with, and among those left in the cupboard, she stuffed crumpled paper and rags, to hold them snug. Poppy nailed boards over the glass doors, so they wouldn't break. He wedged the clock in a tight corner. India Rose lifted from the wall the framed photograph of Abraham Lincoln, seated in his big chair at the Lincoln Memorial temple in Washington, D.C. All the children helped to carry things up from the cellar. Little Joe wrapped the dictionary in a soft cloth. The dictionary belonged to Mommy.

One Friday, exactly ninety-six days ago, after she had done her weekly cleaning for Mrs. Tom Sargent, Mommy had gone to Hoytville's stationer's shop. She had walked in, small, but proud, without saying a thing to anyone beforehand. When she came home, she was carrying the dictionary. It was heavy and fat. It was heavy with words. It was fat with many, many words. Next to Poppy, Little Joe, India Rose, Pearlie May, and Abraham Lincoln, Mommy loved her dictionary.

Every day since then, Mommy had read a page to her family. Sometimes, in her eagerness, Mommy would peep ahead, and read out a word that seemed to speak to her with a special meaning—strong words like *sorrow* and *sacrifice, freedom* and *thrift:* friendly words like *pleasure* and *neighbor:* easy words and hard words: words the Freeds would learn to understand and love and use: words that would never drop from their lips if they lived to be a hundred years old, like *zoöphyte* or *quincunx.*

But in the course of her nightly reading, Mommy had now reached the bottom of page 96, and the word *birthright.*

"Any right, privilege, or possession to which a person is entitled by birth." Mommy read the definition. Every Freed had to study on it.

THE MOVING

Finally, Poppy said, "It could mean, for one thing, that Mommy's love is your birthright, because you were born her children."

Mommy sparkled. Poppy had said not only a true and lovely thing, but he had made the meaning of *birthright* easy to understand.

And after about four minutes of hard brainwork, Little Joe came out with another thought. "It could mean that America is our birthright, because we were born Americans," said Little Joe.

"*America*—our birthright!" whispered Mommy, and her eyes shone like stars. She closed the book and placed it on the shelf. "However did we get along without a dictionary?" she asked, but more as if she were asking herself, in wonder and reverence.

Now, on the eve of moving, Little Joe wrapped the dictionary. It would be safe when the mules high-tailed it down the road tomorrow.

On Monday, the Freed family was up at daydawn. Breakfast must be over and the fire outened by the time the mover arrived. But breakfast seemed a week away, and still he hadn't come. The children ran themselves weary, outside to gaze anxiously up the street, inside to fret and complain. "He promised. Why doesn't he come?"

"The waiting does give a body the fidgets," sighed Mommy. "You should have gone to school this morning, after all. We thought you'd be so excited, and fret your teachers. You must go this afternoon."

"Mommy! How could we find our way, after school?" cried India Rose. "We've never seen the farm. We'd get lost!"

"I declare!" exclaimed Poppy. "Guess I forgot to tell you that the house-moving won't go fast. Why, even if it is only five miles to the farm, it will take Temple six days, maybe, to get us there. He goes through all sorts of motions, hitching and unhitching the pulleys, lifting and shifting the rollers. And the motions are the same, time after time, 'til it's over and done with at last. So you must go to school until he gets the house out on the country road."

Nearly a week to reach the farm! The children were stunned! They had thought it would be so simple—the house rolling as smooth as butter, the mules loping along, and *swanny!*—maybe getting spry and high-tailing it, *lickety cut!*

"It will take patience, Big-Eyes," Poppy went on. "I'm high-wrought to reach the farm myself. Such fine spring weather for getting the plowing and planting under way! Now, it's past nine, and Temple not here! Plague take it, reckon I'm saddled with the ticklish job of going after the ol' slowpoke!"

But now, plodding stodgily down the street, the mover approached, with his mules and all his gear. He offered no apologies for the delay. He was ugly and squat and enormously strong. His chief business was moving buildings. But on the side, he did light hauling. However, he scorned anything lighter than a refrigerator, preferring the largest and most slippery. Grand pianos were really his favorites. He knew that everyone in Hoytville considered him a most disagreeable old bear. But he gloried in it, and secretly he very much enjoyed the taunts thrown at him as he did his moving and hauling. In his way, he was famous.

Now, he didn't even say "good-morning," but fell glumly to work. Poppy had already pried off the front and back steps and set them inside the house. Temple knocked out the foundation slats with a horrible air of relish, as if he were wilfully destroying property. The two men then slid jacks under the floor joists. It was like jacking up an automobile to change a tire.

Beneath the joists of the lifted house, Temple and Poppy shoved long planks. On the planks they placed rollers made from small round logs. Temple rigged up his gear of ropes and pulleys. The team, hitched to the gear, stood several yards ahead of the house. Between, lay another set of planks and rollers. One of the pulleys was fastened to a tree about opposite the heads of the team.

By this time, Mr. Tom Sargent and many of the mill hands had gathered to watch, and to offer unwanted advice. Old Temple muttered, "I been movin' houses 'fore any of you was dry behind the ears." And he pretended to get towering mad when some one called out, "Why don't you get yourself a tractor, Temple? Your moving would go twice as easy."

"Hand over the dough to buy me a tractor!" yelled Temple. "If you don't like my mules an' my way of movin', you can get outa here!" he bellowed. He gathered up the reins. "Gee up!" The mules strained. The ropes began to slip around the squeaking pulleys. The rollers turned. The cottage shivered, sliding forward. The Big Moving had begun.

Once off the home lot and out on the street, Mommy and the children climbed inside the house. They waved good-bye to Poppy. They looked back to see their old pump standing lonely in the yard. The deserted cellar yawned open to the sky.

The moving went by inches. No wonder it would take almost a week! Temple walked at the side, guiding the mules by means of long reins and harsh cries. Slowly the cottage would trundle off its rollers onto the set in front. *Roll, jolt*—it was not exactly as smooth as butter! Temple would then halt the mules, unhitch the pulley from the tree, and anchor it to another tree or post farther along. Then he would go around and pick up the rollers and planks that were left behind, and move them to the front.

THE MOVING

The whole business of rolling, halting, hitching, and carrying was then repeated.

Slow and tedious as it was, the children were at first all giggles. They heard the kitchen pans rattling softly together, as if they, too, were giggling. Mommy's rocking-chair would travel across the room, by itself, rocking, rocking. When Pearlie May sat on the floor, she squealed, "I rumble." The other children tried it, laughing and squirming to feel the trembling of the turning rollers in their bones. This was better than going to school.

Lunch was fun—cold baked beans and ham—in the moving house. It was entertaining to see the people gather on the sidewalks to watch old Temple work. Dogs ran alongside, barking at the mules. As schoolboys passed, going home for lunch, they cat-called remarks that were meant to be funny, and sometimes were. Little Joe grinned at them. He knew when boys said things for fun, and when they said them for spite.

On the narrower streets automobile drivers would be obliged to back, or to turn around and go another way. Some of them were angry. "I keep calm," lied Temple. "Why don't you, wise guy?" The sidewalk rubbernecks grinned and chuckled. The drivers breathed fire and fury. Some of their hot words concerned the family inside the house. The children hid in corners. It was not exactly their fault that their little house occasionally blocked the way. But as they made themselves small, they felt as they sometimes did—that likely some people wished that folks their color didn't live in Hoytville, or in America, anywhere.

Temple now hung nose-bags of feed for his mules. He himself trudged off, the picture of gloom. One would have believed he was on his way to gobble down poison instead of a fine, hearty lunch. Little Joe, India Rose, and Pearlie May departed unwillingly for school. Mommy locked up the house and went to spend the afternoon with friends.

That evening the moving had reached no farther than the main business section of Hoytville. Against darkness, red lanterns hung fore and aft of the Freed cottage. Ahead, and behind it, flares burned in the street. Everything seemed very strange.

CHAPTER THREE

Ice Cream and Lady Cake

Not knowing exactly where they might find their house seemed adventurous to the three Freed children as they left school the next evening. Adventure? By the time the five o'clock whistles blew, and Temple called a halt and placed the flares, the children were wondering if the moving was so much fun, after all. Rolling, squeaking, jolting, stopping and starting—it all seemed endless. Mommy, who had remained in the house the livelong day, was very weary.

But when Poppy came home, it was like cheers in a parade. Poppy brought paper buckets of hot creamed chicken from *The Wishbone Restaurant*. Poppy served it. He would not allow tired Mommy to turn her hand over. Poppy said, gaily, that he'd never seen such warm, beautiful weather so early in the year, and that he just knew their farm was simply rarin' to go. Poppy made jokes.

"Here are the Freeds, fetched stock still in the·-

most highfalutin' part of town," he joked. "I didn't know that Little Joe and Indy Rose and Pearlie May Freed could afford to live among the swells! Howdy, Big Folks!" Playing-like, Poppy swept a bow to the giggling children.

The mover had indeed left the Freed cottage at the southern edge of Hoytville, in its finest section. On either side of the street, beautiful houses stood in wide, grassy lawns. Almost opposite the stranded cottage arose a massive stone church. It was Poppy who called the children's attention to the words chalked on the outside blackboard. ICE CREAM FESTIVAL. COME ONE. COME ALL. Bright paper lanterns were strung on wires from tree to tree. Suddenly it seemed altogether delightful that Temple should have left three little travelers at a place where there was going to be a big party.

"Shall we come one, come all, to the festibul?" asked Pearlie May.

" 'Course not, Honey," laughed Poppy, in his easy, slow way. "This is white folks' festival. But there's not a minikin of harm if my young 'uns want to watch the goings-on."

The children stationed themselves at the front window. Now some ladies bustled out of the church. Others came, driving cars. All stopped in dismay when they saw the cottage almost blocking the street.

ICE CREAM AND LADY CAKE

Several marched up to the cottage door, their heels clicking.

"The ladies are sure frenzied and franzied," murmured Poppy.

"What's the meaning of halting right in front of our church?" demanded the women. *"Tonight,* when we are having an ice cream festival! It's dreadful. It will spoil everything. Please move on at once."

"We're mighty sorry, ma'am, and ma'am." Poppy's voice was soft and polite. "We'd go on if we could. The mover left us here when the evening whistles blew. We're stuck here 'til morning."

What looks of reproach and despair the church ladies flashed at Big Joe Freed, what scorn at his cottage! And when the husbands arrived, they stood about, solemnly discussing the painful and unexpected turn of events. Such words as "police" and "the county highway department" could be plainly heard. At last two of the husbands drove off in an effort to persuade old Temple to bring his gear and move the house, at least into the next block. But when they returned, they announced, "We couldn't pry Temple from his rocking chair and his evening paper."

"Oh, dear!" The ladies sighed and sighed. "Well, we shall just have to make the best of it."

LADYCAKE FARM

Now, in the evening dusk, the paper lanterns flowered into golden moons. The scene was like that in some wonder tale, thought Pearlie May. She and India Rose and Little Joe gazed, enchanted. They saw the church gentlemen set up small tables on the lawn, here and there. They saw big freezers carried up from the church basement. The ladies sliced the cakes. There were round cakes. There were square and oblong cakes. All were mountain-high with beautiful, rich frostings.

People, young and old, began coming from every direction to the festival. Warned by the burning flares, they stopped their cars. Some backed up and turned around. Some crept cautiously along the narrow space that was left in the road. They parked in the neighboring streets, and came trooping back on foot. They were not nearly as cross as the church ladies had warned they would be. They stood about, or sat at tables, laughing and chattering. They dipped their spoons into the frozen mounds of cream. They held thick slices of cake in their fingers.

Little Joe drooled. Pearlie May sucked her thumb as she had done four years ago when she was a baby. India Rose found a sliver of chewing gum in her pocket. It didn't taste in the least like ice cream and cake.

"I s'pect it's Angel Food and Devil's Food and

ICE CREAM AND LADY CAKE

Spice the ladies have," murmured Mommy, all eyes.
"I reckon they have Lady Cake and White Mountain
and Marble Cake."

Poppy spoke, low and comforting. "We'll have us
a cow on the farm. *Swanny,* our cow will give us
cream so thick 't will take a knife to cut it!"

But for once the children scarcely heard Poppy.
The moments slipped past their usual bed-time.
The moon sailed up into the sky, for all the world
like another bright paper lantern. Little Joe, India
Rose and Pearlie May nodded with sleepiness. Yet
who could sleep with such a beautiful big party
going on, and three little Negroes almost a part of
it? Almost, but not quite.

At last the people began leaving. They flung gay
good-nights into the lantern-lit radiance. The children heard the noise of cars, starting up, pulling
away. They saw the church ladies stacking the
soiled dishes, gathering up the spoons. They heard
happy chatter. "In spite of everything, the festival
was a complete success," chattered the ladies.

Now one of the women was dipping deep into a
freezer. She filled a big bowl with ice cream. She
wrapped half of a big cake in waxed paper. She was
plump, and wore a starched apron. She appeared
to be a person who reveled in good things like cake
and ice cream. "I bet the fat lady is going to take
that left-over ice cream home with her," whispered

Little Joe, his mouth watering. "She will eat that ice cream and that cake all by herself, I bet."

But the plump lady walked across the church lawn, carrying the heaped bowl and the cake. She crossed the sidewalk. She marched right up to the Freeds' front porch. Could this be true? The children stared, as tense and still as bunny rabbits just before they take off into the bushes.

But Mommy went bravely forward. She took the bowl and the package of cake. "Thank you kindly," said Mommy, smiling her shy, pretty smile. Poppy bowed. The shining eyes, the shining white teeth of Little Joe, India Rose and Pearlie May said "thank you" as plainly as words.

The lady turned and left, smiling. India Rose ran for spoons and saucers. Mommy served big helpings of ice cream. She unwrapped and sliced the cake. The frosting was mountain-high. "I s'pect this is White Mountain Cake," said Mommy. She pursed her mouth, as proud as if her own small brown hands had made the beautiful cake.

Little Joe, spoon poised thoughtfully, gazed after the kind, plump woman. "I think it's *Lady* Cake," said Little Joe.

"Yes, Son," agreed Mommy, softly. "It's sure-enough *Lady* Cake."

Presently Poppy took the empty bowl back to the church. And while Little Joe, India Rose and

ICE CREAM AND LADY CAKE

Pearlie May, drum-tight with cake and ice cream, fell happily asleep, Poppy helped to wind up the festival. He carried tables into the church basement. Freezers and folding chairs he carried. He gathered up scattered paper napkins.

"Thank you kindly," said all the smiling church ladies to Big Joe Freed.

So at last the festival was over. The golden lanterns shone no more. The church grounds stretched clean and empty. All of the workers, women and men, went home. The fine big houses slept in their lawns. The humble Freed cottage slept in the silent street.

But in the spring moonlight the words chalked on the church blackboard seemed to glow with a faint and lovely shine. ICE CREAM FESTIVAL. COME ONE. COME ALL.

CHAPTER FOUR

Bittersweet

When the moving reached the country roads, the Freed children left their Hoytville school for good. They played along the rural roadsides. They explored the borders of unfenced meadows. There was never the least danger of the caravan speeding up and leaving them in the lurch. They could always catch up with it. Why, they even ran ahead, and waited, full of mischief, playing a joke on the cottage! "Hurry up, you old slowpoke of a house!" they called out, softly. They couldn't risk Temple hearing them. They were still half-afraid of him.

On Saturday morning Poppy didn't go to the mill in Hoytville. Instead, he rode his bike to the farm, with gleeful Little Joe perched on the handle bars. For Temple had promised, grudgingly, that he would reach the farm by noonday.

It was wonderful to see Poppy and Little Joe waiting, when the caravan arrived. The farm, at last! Neglected and weedy, it was not yet much to look at. But there was such hope and happiness in the hearts of its new owners that it seemed the most beautiful farm on earth. And was ever April day so bright?

The grass-grown lane was flanked by tall locust. trees. There was the sad, scarred place where once had stood the farmhouse which had burned. Right away, Mommy said if Poppy would plow it up, she would plant her flower garden there. In place of scars there would be blossoms.

Poppy and the mover, after much work and a long time, got the cottage settled on its new foundations. Old Temple, with fresh pay in his pocket, plodded off toward Hoytville. That's the last we shall see of him. Good riddance, too!

The Freeds now fell valiantly to work. The best dishes were unpacked and shelved. The cupboards were made orderly. Abraham Lincoln was hung on the wall. The dictionary, unwrapped and on its shelf again, had not a scratch on it. Poppy and Little Joe connected the stove pipe and kindled a fire. While Mommy started a hot supper, the girls redded up the rooms. They looked the same as in Hoytville.

But the indoors didn't seem to matter greatly, now that so much glorious outdoors belonged to the Freeds. That wide sky over those forty spreading acres—*their* acres! *Their* friendly big maple tree— it was all that Poppy had promised. The tree was so splendid that it lent beauty to the little cottage which it sheltered. It was just putting forth its rosy, wrinkled new leaves. That night, the weary children, looking up and up, saw how the the half-bare boughs seemed to be hung with sparkling stars. "It dizzies me," said Pearlie May, blinking.

"We Freeds can't be anything but enduring good," declared Mommy, "keeping company with a tree so noble tall it carries the stars."

The next morning ushered in a high, windy day, one minute spring-bright, the next as gray as winter. The family set out for a tour of the farm. Near the site of the former house, blooming daffodils gleamed amid rank grass, like half-buried gold. A twisty old grape-vine was sending forth delicate pink tendrils over a trellis black with age. In fence corners clumps of rhubarb and asparagus were up. The garden wilderness was bordered with wiry brambles which Poppy said were raspberry canes.

"Everything needs pruning," said Poppy. He flexed his arms. The big muscles bunched up, hard. Mommy's laughter rang out like chimes. "All that we do on our farm we shall do with joy, because it's ours," she cried.

"Look!" caroled Pearlie May, pointing at three blossoming plum trees. "They are posy vases set out by Somebody, to smarten up the farm."

"And oh-hhh, *smell!*" India Rose ran closer. The fragrance of the blossoms made the children breathe so deeply their toes curled. They cavorted and skipped. They were half-crazy with joy—forty acres of joy!

Little Joe shinned up one of the squat old apple trees, now going thorny with neglect. "With trimming and spraying," remarked Poppy, "we may have some good apples, in time. Bringing this farm back to yield will take a shuck of work."

"I'll work, body and britches!" shouted Little Joe, boiling over with brave intentions. He turned a jolly cartwheel when Poppy said, "You children will whitewash this old henhouse, and ready it for the hens to live clean."

"Won't we jus' slap on that whitewash?" cried India Rose.

"This woodlot is something I'm plenty proud of," declared Poppy, leading his family on. "Into these woods we'll sometimes turn our pigs and chickens, to root and scratch. As soon as I wire the house and do a million other chores, I'll chop out the dead wood and the poorer trees. It's many a fence post we'll have out of here, and we'll stack up cordwood for Mommy's cooking fire. We'll not let a smidgen of anything go to waste, if it can be helped."

India Rose rushed to fondle Poppy's hand. Oh, her poppy would work miracles on this farm!

"And listen!" whispered Mommy. "We have song-tunes in our woodlot."

Birds flew above the dusky aisles, warbling their

spring melodies. Rabbits jumped from under the very feet of the Freeds. Squirrels skittered and scolded. A covey of baby quail scuttled away so fast they made the head swim. Little Joe was certain he saw a 'coon. "A wild animal woods of our own!" he whispered. His sisters, silent with awed delight, walked tippytoed.

The family returned to the cottage for a rest, and a bite of lunch. Afterward they roamed the hummocky fields and pastures which had forgotten the plow and the harrow. The children squealed with joy when they discovered a small brook flowing through the far pasture. It was talking to itself. For so long there had been no one to hear. But now, with three happy children to listen, it would bubble over with merry chatter. When they dipped their fingers in its bright ripples, they found it ice-cold.

And then, at the southwestern edge of the pasture, they saw the high fence of barbed wire. They knew, by the peeled posts and shiny wire, that it was a brand-new fence. The barbs looked cruel in the spring light. And they were cruel. For on one of the posts was tacked a fresh shingle, and on the shingle were painted these words, "Niggers unwelcome. Keep out."

They read the words. Poppy and Mommy, Pearlie May, India Rose, and Little Joe read the words, each to himself, in silence. Poppy's left hand reached for

BITTERSWEET

Mommy's hand. His right hand took one of India Rose's. Mommy held Little Joe's hand, tight. Little Joe clasped the small fingers of Pearlie May. They stood strung out there in the field, hand in hand, reading the cruel words.

Clouds scudded across the sky, hiding the sun. The day was suddenly as gray as winter. A cold wind blew over the ragged, dun fields. Mommy shivered. The Freeds turned, stricken and wordless, plodding toward the house.

At last Poppy spoke. " 'T isn't Lady Cake—that sign. But don't you all mind. The land on the other side of the barbs belongs to Mr. Mort Carle. He and his unmarried son, Bob, work it. It's the best farm around. It's five times the acreage we've got. They call it *Golden Grain Farm*. A pretty name like that —you'd think Carle would be a soft-hearted guy. Maybe 't was his wife thought it up. But, anyway, Carle was the one man who told Tom Sargent we wouldn't be welcome here. Now he's shown it, in plain words on the shingle. 'T isn't Lady Cake, but don't you all mind. Don't *you* mind, dear Mommy."

"We'll stay quiet on our side, and we'll take joy in our farm," announced Mommy. Her mouth trembled, but she held her head high. "We'll take joy," she repeated, "same as the birds take joy in our woodlot, same as our maple tree takes joy in sun and rain, in winter and summer. Don't you mind, Chickies." Through the tears on her lashes, Mommy smiled down at her children.

"It's turned fresh cold," she said. "We'll stir up the fire and the house will be snug. I'll cook a nice hot meal. Afterward we'll read a page." Mommy's voice, which had been sharp with pain, mellowed. " 'Count of moving, we haven't read the dictionary for nigh a week."

The cottage was snug and warm. Mommy fried bacon and potatoes. She baked corn dodger. Tomatoes out of a can were made tasty with butter, sugar, nutmeg, and bits of toast. After a long trudge over the fields, the supper was very good. Then Mommy read page 97 from the dictionary. The final word was *bittersweet.*

"*Bittersweet. Mingled sweetness and bitterness,* or, *pleasure and pain,*" read Mommy.

They studied over the meaning, as Mommy had taught them to do.

India Rose was the first to respond. " 'Pleasure and pain,' like today. Maybe like today," said India Rose, shyly.

The day lived again in their minds—pleasure in plum blossom and bird song and a brook—pain in barbed wire and cruel words.

"Surely like today," answered Mommy. She gave a small sigh as she turned back to the book. "But 'mingled pain and pleasure' is not the only meaning of *bittersweet*," she said. "It means also 'a twining shrub with small greenish flowers and clusters of fruit, which ripen in the fall and burst open, displaying scarlet covered seeds.' "

"I saw the same, twining on some of our fences today," Poppy said. "Bittersweet is beauty-bright when its time comes. Next fall, we'll gather our bittersweet. Mommy and the girls can make it up into bunches. Your teachers will fancy it. P'raps Indy Rose and Little Joe might sell some bunches in Hoytville. Or, maybe before that I'll put up a roadside stand. Maybe we'll sell things—tomatoes an' beans, sweet corn and squashes, posy bunches, and in the fall, the bittersweet."

Little Joe, lying on the floor the better to listen, kicked up his heels at such wonderful prospects. India Rose felt like doing a jiggety-jig. Instead, she folded her hands in her lap, as primly as a little old lady in lace mitts. Said India Rose, "It will give us much pleasure, Poppy, to sell the bittersweet."

Poppy and Mommy exchanged twinkles of pride. "It's the dictionary working in Indy Rose makes her talk so nice," Poppy decided.

"Maybe by the time we've reached page 600, all of us will be talking nice all the while," Mommy said. She took a deep breath. Then she added, calmly, "I wouldn't be s'prised if this dictionary won't pave the way for Indy Rose and Little Joe and

Pearlie May to go to college when they're the right age and have worked hard enough to make the farm pay."

The mouths of the children fell open. Out of her quiet, their mommy did say the most amazing things!

"Once-upon-a-time we're all going to college," agreed Pearlie May, breathlessly. Oh, yes, going to college would be a real wonder story for the Freeds!

"*Jubilee!*" cried Poppy. He stood up, tall, and swelled out his chest. He gave it a hard whack with his fist. "We'll make the farm pay! Of course we will!" he thundered. "But not by staying up late and dawdling of mornings. So off to bed, every one of us!" Poppy gave the children mock spanks, as they scampered past him, squealing with laughter.

In the night, Little Joe wakened, an unheard-of thing for such a healthy boy. Perhaps it was the strangeness of sleeping in the country, so large and still. Little Joe lay thinking. There were pleasant words and there were painful words. Now, in the night, no one, white-skinned or dark, could see the ugly words painted on the shingle. But they were there, beyond the happy, uncaring brook, and they'd show up by daylight. The memory of them troubled Little Joe so much that at last he tiptoed through the house to stand by Mommy's bed. He didn't call her, or touch her, but she turned on her pillow and saw him. She did not ask what troubled him, nor did he say, but she knew. She got up, quickly. She drew Little Joe to the front window, pointing to the big maple tree, calm and majestic, rooted so firmly in the dark, fertile earth.

Then she took the boy back to his own bed, and tucked him in. She sat by him, her hand on his, until he fell asleep.

CHAPTER FIVE

Good Neighbors

Before leaving Hoytville, Poppy had arranged with the superintendent to enter Little Joe, India Rose and Pearlie May in their new school. But he told the children they might stay at home their first week in the country. "I want to go myself, beforehand, and talk to the principal. Up to now I haven't had time."

The following Wednesday Poppy visited the school. When he returned he said the school bus would pick up the children the next Monday morning, and that the books were the same as in Hoytville. "It is called the New Hope Township School," Poppy reported. "There are eight grades. Ninety-nine children attend. The principal, Miss Johnson, seemed mighty pleasant," Poppy went on. "She said you Freeds would be welcome, and she took me around and named me to your teachers. I promised 'em," warned Poppy, "that they wouldn't have any trouble with you. I told 'em Little Joe is a good boy with generally a grin on his face. And I said that Pearlie May could sing like a bird in a tree."

GOOD NEIGHBORS

India Rose waited. Her hair-ribbons quivered.

"And I told the teacher," Poppy said, grinning fondly down at his eldest daughter, "that Indy Rose is named for Mrs. Tom Sargent. I said, 'Indy Rose is clever at speaking pieces, 'specially out of the book Mis' Sargent gave 'er.'"

India Rose reached for the book, hugging it to her. "Poppy, you could 've said that the name of my book is *I Love Poetry*." Then she added, cautiously, "Any others like us at New Hope School?"

"You're the only ones," Poppy answered. "You and Pearlie May are not so likely to have any trouble, but you might listen to what I say to your brother."

"Little Joe," Poppy began, "when you get on that bus next Monday morning, and all the time at school, you keep square an' steady on your feet. Keep your hands to yourself, forevermore. And no matter what, you keep your grin on your face. Maybe you'll get plum' tired o' that grin before the school boys quit their tormenting and take up with you. But don't you get tired of your grin 'til they get tired of their tormenting."

"Okay," promised Little Joe, steadily. School was still four days distant.

"You can take off your grin, Son, and rest your face, once you're home safe and sound," said Mommy.

In the meantime, Poppy patched up the rickety barn. He did it against the advice of Tom Sargent, who had from the beginning taken a friendly interest in the Freed farm. "The first big blow comes along, that old wreck will surely flatten out," warned Mr. Tom. "Better build a new barn, Big Joe. I'll let you have the lumber at cost. Pay for it when you can."

"That's everlasting kind of you, Mr. Tom," answered Poppy. "A big blow isn't likely. This barn must stand 'til fall, when I'll try to get a new one built against the winter cold. I've got a slew of needments to buy, an' I don't fancy going into debt any deeper 'n I can help."

Poppy and Little Joe cleaned out the musty old stalls. Right away some animals came to live in them. First came a cow. India Rose and Pearlie May named her Violet. For now, in April, weren't there the prettiest velvety violets blooming in fence corners, along the brook, and in the woodlot? *Their* violets for the picking; *their* cow for the milking! And whoever tasted such milk and cream and butter? Violet the cow was a Grade A dairy plant in herself—*The Violet Freed Dairy.*

Poppy bought a horse. Little Joe was so vasty proud of that horse, he named him *High-Stepper*, although the creature was a clumsy slow-poke, with heavy slow-come feet. A mule, which came ready-named as *Levi,* and refused, mulishly, to answer to any name more frivolous, was bought to team up with High-Stepper. From the first, the pair were chums.

Poppy said that some sweet day, when the money came to his hand, he would own a tractor and be a sure-enough modern farmer. But until then he would do with an old-fashioned plow. By scouting around, Poppy was able to get a wooden-beam walking plow. The farmer who owned it, said, "That plow has been standing in the shed ever since I bought a tractor two years ago. I been intending to hand it over to the junk man. You can have the plow for the taking," the farmer told Poppy. "It will be okay, once you get the points sharpened up."

Poppy plowed up the garden patch. He leveled it off with the aid of High-Stepper and a log drag, while all the neighborhood robins followed, feasting on the delicious angleworms turned up by the plow. Mommy and the girls planted the first seeds out of paper packets.

With old brooms the children whitewashed the garage, screaming with laughter when their bare feet and ankles turned into white boots. "We're to keep our tools in this old garage," Little Joe explained to his sisters, "and maybe our wagon, when we get one." They whitewashed the chicken house. Poppy and Mommy and Little Joe strung shiny new wire around the chicken lot.

Poppy rode his bike into town, where he selected a dozen hens at the Hoytville Feed and Poultry House. The hens and some bags of feed were delivered the next day. Pearlie May had expected *clouds* of hens! Poppy grinned, saying, "We start small with everything, Honey. These hens will lay eggs for our own use. But just you have patience, Child. There's nothing works so wonderful as Nature. This hen-flock will largen. Later we'll have our own cabbages and clover and grain, an' such, to help out on feed."

On Friday Poppy fell to talking over the fence with Mr. Jim Cummings, who owned the farm to the east called *Grassy Acres.* It turned out that Mr. Cummings was a man who dearly loved to give advice. That which he handed over the fence to Poppy, free of charge, was very good indeed. After talking with Cummings, Poppy returned to the cottage fairly walking on air.

"What do you know!" cried Poppy. "Mr. Cummings says he has a wagon I can buy at a fair price, if I favor it. I'm to go over this evening and look it over. I sure do need a wagon. Mr. Cummings says he has a two-horse harrow I can have. It needs some new teeth, he says. But I can find teeth, an' not out of Little Joe's mouth, either," joked Poppy, full of high spirits. "Mr. Cummings says he knows where

I can get a corn-planter second-hand, and that I should be able to pick up a cultivator somewhere." Poppy's eyes twinkled, as he went on about the new neighbor. "Mr. Cummings looked me over, pretty sharp, and then he said, 'We're used to swapping work and machinery around here. You look plenty hefty for work.'

" 'I don't want to seem braggy,' I answered Mr. Cummings, 'but Man, I'm plenty hefty!' So then I got up my dare, and I said, 'It's a ticklish subject, sir, but you know I can never swap my work for any of Mr. Carle's machinery. He's not neighborly like you, sir. He can't abide me and mine. He's put up a sign and barbed wire, saying so.'

"Cummings nodded. 'Sounds like Mort Carle, all right,' he said. 'Carle's a master farmer, but a stiff-necked sort of fellow, once he's set his mind against a thing. Keep to yourself with him, Big Joe. He's not likely to do you actual harm, I'd say.' "

That evening, leading Levi, Poppy set out for the Cummings farm to have a look at the wagon and the harrow. The children didn't ask to go, in so many words, but their eyes begged.

" 'T wouldn't do, all of you storming in on new neighbors when maybe they don't fancy pigtails." Poppy tweaked his daughter's braids. "But we can try 'em out on one set of pigtails. Suppose you draw straws."

Mommy held broom straws, while the children drew. India Rose was the lucky one. Poppy allowed her to ride on Levi's back. When they arrived at Grassy Acres, and Poppy had lifted her down, it was all India Rose could do to keep her face straight and to mind her manners. She had to hold herself tight, so that her joy would not swell full-blown about a thing which might not turn out to a little girl's liking. Yet she couldn't help feeling "balloonish" when Judy Cummings stood before her. Judy was a child with pigtails and freckles. She was just the age of India Rose. She invited her caller to push her in the rope swing, and India Rose pushed with great goodwill. Said Judy to India Rose, "You have a pretty name. I have a doll named *Rose.*" And when she heard about Pearlie May, Judy said, "Your sister has a pretty name, too. Maybe, if Mother will let me, I will come over some Saturday and play with you and Pearlie May."

Going back home, Poppy and India Rose sat high and proud behind Levi on the seat of the wagon which Poppy had bought from Mr. Jim Cummings. In the wagon bed the second-hand harrow lay upside down, its spike teeth pointed upward. *Their* wagon! *Their* harrow! *Glory,* Poppy and India Rose felt as if flags should be flying and drums thumping! Even Levi seemed to walk with a jauntier step, as if cockades nodded elegantly at his funny, tall ears.

GOOD NEIGHBORS

Clutched preciously to her chest, India Rose carried a glass of plum jelly. Mrs. Cummings was sending it to Mommy as a gift. The jelly was the color of the rarest ruby. Mommy set it against the light, so that she could see it glowing ruby-red through the evening hours. The Freeds had not been so happy since they had first come to the farm and seen the stars hanging in their maple tree.

"It's sure Lady Cake, having such kindly neighbors as the Cummings," declared Poppy.

Poppy had taken a great fancy, ever since the night of the ice-cream-and-cake festival, for saying that things were like Lady Cake, or not like Lady Cake.

CHAPTER SIX

A Nice Monday Morning

By Saturday Little Joe was beginning to think often and uneasily about the school bus stopping for the young Freeds. "Poppy, there are only a few weeks of school left," he remarked in an off-hand, but practical manner. "Seems hardly worth while going for such a short time."

"School's important, as long as school keeps," answered Poppy.

On Sunday morning Little Joe declared, "It's too bad, when there's so much to be done getting the farm started, that you must do without my help."

"Too bad you're not twins," Poppy said, "one of you a *greeny*, with no mind 'cept for grubbin'; the other, Little Joe Freed who's going to college some day."

On Sunday evening Little Joe mourned, "Levi and High-Stepper and Vi'let are going to miss me like sixty."

"You will brush Levi and High-Stepper of evenings," Poppy assured him. "You will carry in the pails of evening milk."

There was no stopping Time. Monday morning came. The children waited out front, so clean they looked splinter-new. Little Joe had butterflies in his stomach. India Rose's eyes were big and solemn. Pearlie May's eyes were big, too, but bright with supreme faith that school would be nice.

The bus, when it drew up full of youngsters, was not so much a bus, as Bedlam-on-wheels. If neither the driver nor the passengers knew what *Bedlam* meant, Little Joe, India Rose and Pearlie May Freed could have told them. They had made the acquaintance of this word some three weeks ago, on page 84 of Mommy's dictionary. *Bedlam, a madhouse:* hence, *any scene of uproar and confusion.*

But as the three children mounted the steps and entered, the uproar died away into complete silence. The staring moon faces and the silence of the passengers made the Freeds feel all legs and feet. India Rose and Pearlie May sank, as one child, into a very small space. What a relief when *Bedlam* began to rise again on a wave of whispers, giggles and shrill meaningless cries! The mounting uproar was due partly to unquenchable spirits. But it was also due to the fact that when Little Joe started to slide into a vacant place, it closed up at once. He tried again. The same thing happened.

Little Joe remembered, then, what Poppy had told him. Little Joe's grin was never very far away. Now he called it, and it came. His mouth spread. His white teeth shone. His eyes brightened. He kept his hands to himself. He braced himself squarely and steadily. Grinning, Little Joe stood the remaining two miles to the schoolhouse. Time and again the boys moved aside, pretending to make room for him, and welcome. But he knew they would play the same prank. So Little Joe let on that a standing position was his favorite way of riding in a school bus. Little Joe made out as if he wouldn't sit down, even if he had his choice of any seat, from front to back.

The driver kept one eye on the road, and one on his mirror, watching to see that his passengers did not carry their welcome of this new boy too far. "Looks as if he could take care of himself," thought the driver. "Doggone if his grin isn't as catching as measles! Makes *me* grin, even on a Monday morning!" Chuckling, the driver pulled up in the yard of New Hope School. The children scrambled pell-mell, out of the bus. As Little Joe alighted, a sly foot slid out and tripped him. He fell flat on his face. But he was up again, quicker than a Jack-in-the-box.

Judy Cummings, who had not gathered quite enough spunk to show friendship on the bus, now

offered to escort India Rose and Pearlie May to the
principal's office. Three girl friends of Judy's smiled
and said, "Hello-what's-your-name?"—a greeting
which Poppy would have said was as nice as Lady
Cake.

Little Joe followed at a distance, not wishing to
be seen with girls, only. He took in the two-story,
red brick schoolhouse at a glance. There was an out-
door playground and a ball field. Parking space allowed room for the buses to turn around, and for
the teachers' cars. The thing that made this schoolhouse different from any Little Joe had ever seen
were the farm fields and meadows marching right
up to its edges. It was a real country school, all
righty, and just the place for a farm boy, as long as
school kept. Little Joe knew that some day, when
the other boys had accepted him, he would like it
here. He trudged inside, not exactly cheerful, but
not in the dumps, either.

Judy Cummings left the Freeds at the open door
of the office. From her desk a kind-faced lady beck-
oned. "Welcome, children," she said. "I am Miss
Johnson, the principal."

"It's a pleasure to meet you, Miss Johnsing,"
answered India Rose. Pearlie May gave a quick bob
and murmured "pleasure" in faint echo. Little Joe
scraped his foot and looked as bright as he could
manage.

From among her papers the principal picked up the report cards from the Hoytville school. She read aloud. "Joseph Booker Freed, Grade 6B. India Rose Freed, 4A. Pearlie May Freed, 2B. Those are nice names you have," remarked Miss Johnson, smiling.

"It's a pleasure to know you like them, Miss John-sing," beamed India Rose.

"Well!" exclaimed Miss Johnson. "I do think you talk very nicely indeed."

"Thank you kin'ly. It's the dictionary makes us talk nice," stated India Rose.

"The dictionary?" queried Miss Johnson.

"It's Mommy's dictionary." Pearlie May couldn't keep still a moment longer. She shone across at the principal. "Our mommy reads the dictionary to us, evenings. We're a-going to college."

Little Joe fidgeted, uneasily. Maybe his sisters were chattering too much. Maybe their chatter was causing Miss Johnson to laugh, inside her white-folks self.

But inside herself, a bird of joy which used to sing to Miss Johnson when she was a young, inspired teacher fresh from training, was at this moment warbling again the bright song she had almost forgotten.

Gazing at those three dark pansy faces across from her—pansy-velvet skin, pansy-velvet eyes, Miss Johnson was silent, listening to that bird of her youth, piping a fresh new Monday morning into her school routine. She took off her glasses, wiping them with her handkerchief. She put them on again, and when she could speak for the sudden lump in her throat, she exclaimed, softly, "A dictionary, evenings! College! Oh, you trusting three! Why, the hope and future of your race lies in education! The hope and future of the world, whatever the race, whatever the country! Within my power, you three *will* go to college!" For a moment Miss Johnson's mouth and eyes had a fierce, fighting look. Then, drawing a long breath, she relaxed. "We've never had any colored children in this school," she said, in a cheerful, honest way. "But you're very welcome here. In fact," added Miss Johnson, "you've made this the nicest Monday morning I've had in years."

That evening the boys on the school bus again tempted Little Joe to take a seat. He wished he could fight 'em. But Poppy had told him to keep his fists to himself. Again he stood up the two miles. When he reached home, he didn't take off his grin to rest his aching cheeks, because his mother looked at him so searchingly and anxiously. "New Hope School is fine, Mommy," he assured her, and he showed all his white teeth.

"I'm certain sure school will be fine some day, even as I'm sure it is not fine yet, Little Joe," she said, after Pearlie May had related all that had been said in Miss Johnson's office. "The principal of New Hope School is on your side," Mommy rejoiced. "The principal is *for* you!"

"What did Miss Johnsing mean, Mommy and Poppy, when she said we'd made her such a nice Monday morning?" asked Pearlie May.

"I wouldn't know exactly what she meant, less'n I'd been there myself an' heard her," Poppy answered. "But I think it's the same as Lady Cake to Miss Johnson, having three pretty-mannered youngsters come to her school and tell they read a dictionary, regular, and want to go to college. An' maybe," added Poppy, thoughtfully, "it means an extra special Lady Cake to Miss Johnson, when she knows those youngsters will have to work harder than most for what they make of themselves."

"You and your *Lady Cake*, Poppy!" laughed Mommy, tremulously. "But he's right, Chickies. That's why you made a nice Monday morning for Miss Johnson."

Little Joe didn't say anything. A nice Monday morning? It had been quite nice in Miss Johnson's office. It had not been nice on the school bus, neither morning nor evening. "I s'pec it will take a while 'fore it's nice the whole time," reflected Little Joe. He took off his grin and hid it under his pillow, until morning.

CHAPTER SEVEN

School and Home

All of that first week, going and coming, Little Joe Freed was obliged to stand up. His sisters never told at home, and the driver did nothing about it. To save himself from going to the madhouse, the driver had learned not to bother too much with the Bedlam inside the bus, as long as the children seemed in no danger of being torn limb from limb. "Little Joe is bound to win, if he can just keep wearing that grin long enough," the driver told himself. "I can see how the boys can hardly hold out against that grin."

But first, something else happened. The next Monday morning, to the surprise of the Bedlamites, the driver stopped in front of the Carle place, where a girl stood waiting. Her brightly scarfed head blocked out part of the name on the fancy sign be-hind her—*Golden Grain Farm*. There were neither children nor grandchildren at Golden Grain Farm. Then, who could this girl be?

The uproar in the bus quieted as the strange girl entered. And at that moment, while the children stared at her, Little Joe Freed slipped quickly into a seat. When it was discovered, the boys nearest him bumped shoulders with him, and they kicked his shins. But the bumps and kicks were friendly. The boys were openly pleased with Little Joe for outwitting them when they weren't looking. Little Joe's grin was never so natural, and small *hallelujahs,* secret but joyous, shouted within India Rose and Pearlie May. The tormenting of Little Joe had come to an end. All of the passengers turned their attention to the new girl.

She looked like any other eleven-year-old girl. But she talked funny. Her name was Mirzda Dorbe, which had a strange, foreign sound. She said, "I am what you call D.P. But no! Vunce I am 'Displaced Person,' but now I American like you. My father— he come work for Mr. Carle. My mother come. All come. We are leaving our country because of Communists. We lose our home. We lose our money. Everything we are losing. When we leave our home like hurry we have only the clothes on our backs." Mirzda smiled, cheerfully. She had but faint memory of that dreadful flight.

All of the New Hope schoolgirls wanted to be friends with Mirzda Dorbe, who had come from a strange country across the sea. India Rose and Pearlie May wanted to be friends, too. But they were used to holding back until they knew whether the cold shoulder would be turned on them, or the smiling look. Mirzda—living now at Golden Grain Farm—did Mirzda know about that sign Mr. Carle had tacked on the barbed wire fence? Had she read the cruel words? Would Mirzda, new to American ways, think of India Rose and Pearlie May as two little human beings branded with a cruel and ugly name?

After school they told Mommy and Poppy about Mirzda.

"At 'sembly this morning Miss Johnsing told about the different kind of people who came to New Hope School lately," reported India Rose. "She meant us, and Mirzda who lives at the Carle place. With her mouth Miss Johnsing made her words round and careful, so that all the kids would understand. She said, 'It is nice for this school to have such int'ressing new pupils. Now we are all Americans together, here in this school we love. Mirzda Dorbe is an American because America reached out and gave her leave to live in this country, in safety and at peace. Her native country now lies behind the Iron Curtain, which is actually barbed wire stretched along the borders of the tyrant land.'

"And Mommy," India Rose went on, "Miss Johnsing said, 'The Freed children, Joseph, India Rose, and Pearlie May are birthright Americans, just as you and I. Never forget that these new pupils are Americans, who have the same rights and duties that you have. Mirzda and Joseph, India Rose and Pearlie May, we make you very welcome at New Hope School.' That's what Miss Johnsing said," finished India Rose.

"How ever nice!" murmured Mommy. "And it's sorry we are for the little D.P. girl. Maybe the home she was turned out of could 've been a nice farm, like ours."

"Wait 'til you hear, Mommy." Pearlie May sucked in her breath, as she did when she had something important to say. "At recess we played in a ring. And Mirzda the D.P. girl wouldn't catch hold of my hand. She didn't say anything, and her face didn't look mad. But she moved to another place, so she wouldn't have to touch my hand."

Poppy got up suddenly, and strode off to the barn. But Mommy said, "Mirzda lives at the Carle place. So she's bound to mis-reckon us, same as the Carles do. You children are old enough to know that often brown hand and white hand won't touch. Sometimes it's the brown hand that's ready to take hurt beyond all reason. Sometimes it's the white hand, scorning the brown hand as unworthy. Don't you sicken your marrows about things like that, but go your own way, proper-mannered and stout-hearted. We've got the farm to gladden us, and our trust in the dictionary, and being Americans, like Miss Johnson said. . . . Our new pig came today. Run out to the pen and tell her 'howdy-do.' "

SCHOOL AND HOME

The pig was white all over, except for a black belt encircling her plump middle. The belt was as neat and even as though it had been painted on with the aid of a tapeline. The pig and her belt made the children laugh. Then and there, they named her *Fatty*, which is a good name for any self-respecting and respected pig.

Now there was a horse and a mule, chickens and a pig. A yellow cat came from somewhere, having smelled out the *Violet Freed Grade A Dairy*. Pearlie May named the cat *Cinderella*. It made no difference to Pearlie May that Cinderella was a boy cat.

One evening Jim Cummings drove his car into the Freeds' lane. On the front seat with him sat Judy, her eyes dancing-bright, and with good reason. For in a basket, nestled in straw and covered warmly, were two new-born lambs.

"Spring's so early and the work crowding me," explained Jim Cummings. "I can't fool with these weaklings. Wife doesn't fancy bothering with them, either. It's the nature of a ewe, sometimes to get cranky and imagine that one of her babies doesn't smell like it's hers. When that happens the fool mother won't have a thing to do with the kid. If you Freeds want to nurse these along by hand and keep them, you're welcome."

"I'll be swandoogled!" exclaimed Poppy, unable to use tame, ordinary words, while the other Freeds gazed open-mouthed at the shaky new lambs. Then, when they were able to speak, they knew that a mere "thank-you" was not big enough, nor dazzling enough, to offer their neighbors. But Mr. Cummings and Judy seemed to understand. When they had driven away, Little Joe borrowed Poppy's pet expression, crying out, "It's Lady Cake, getting the lambs!"

"It's a break!" agreed Poppy. "Bottle-feeding the lambs will be a care. But watch us work at it, every one of us!"

There was no end to the farm work. While the children were at school, their parents toiled the livelong day. Before and after school and on Saturdays the children worked. They fed the lambs and the hens and Fatty the pig. India Rose and Little Joe learned to milk. Little Joe curried the team, although not every day. One evening during Holy Week, Poppy and Little Joe cut potatoes for planting, while the girls did the dishes and Mommy began on the C-words in the dictionary. Mommy did her Friday cleaning for Mrs. Sargent on Thursday that week, because every one knows that early potatoes must be planted on Good Friday—or *else!* Poppy and Mommy planted their early potatoes on Good Friday.

Every silly hen became frenzied and franzied to raise a family. Even over one lone egg, she had to be pried off her nest. Mommy allowed three hens to brood settings which Poppy brought from the Hoyt-ville Poultry and Feed Shop. The patience of those setting hens! They might have been china hens, on china baskets! But how they carried on when the chickens hatched! And how Pearlie May and India Rose loved those downy balls of new life! It was wonderful, how the farm increased!

But one of the lambs died. Pearlie May cried until her cheeks swelled out even with her eyes, and India Rose and Little Joe had to keep their upper lips stiff. Poppy said that such things happen. "Farmer folk can only do their best. We did our best with the lamb. Let's be thankful that the other one is healthy."

At school, after the boys had gulped down their lunches in large, unchewed chunks, they played baseball. Little Joe sat on the sidelines and watched. How Mommy knew that her son was merely a looker-on, he could not have guessed. But on one of her Fridays in Hoytville, Mommy bought a base-ball for Little Joe. He took it to school. After noon recess, he managed to walk into the schoolhouse with the fellow who was playing third base that week. Said Little Joe, off-hand, but with his best grin, "I'm not braggin', but I made more than one grand slam home run in Hoytville."

So Little Joe was invited to play. He was not such a veteran at pitching and catching, but *boy,* when

he spit on his hands and swung that bat! And *boy,*
Little Joe could ankle around that diamond, catch
up with the flying ball, and hit the dirt at the plate
as fast as anybody at New Hope School had ever
done it! What if he did scrape off several inches of
skin, sliding to base? The kids whistled and cheered.
"Pee Wee! Pee Wee!" they screamed. In a way,
getting nicknamed *Pee Wee* by his schoolmates
meant as much to Little Joe as though he were a
famous professional, being asked to autograph base-
balls.

Moreover, when Little Joe's teacher asked her pupils to write compositions about any subject they
chose, Little Joe wrote one called *Why Schoolchil-
dren Like Sports.* He was invited to read it before
the class, and he was proud to do it, because it bore
a grade of *Excellent.* The teacher, it seemed, was
quite amazed that Joseph Booker Freed had used
grown-up words so suitable to a work on sports, such
as *ambition* and *athletic, booster, contest,* and *cele-
brated.* But at home Mommy said, quietly, "It's the
dictionary working in Little Joe makes him write
so stylish." That evening she began reading two
pages at a sitting, instead of one.

It happened that the very next day Miss Johnson
entered, one after another, the rooms of the upper
grades. In Little Joe's 6B room, his teacher stepped
aside, so that Miss Johnson could talk.

SCHOOL AND HOME

"The American Legion of this state is offering three prizes to the pupils of the sixth through the eighth grades who write the best essays on American citizenship," announced Miss Johnson. "The contestants may handle this subject in whatever way they wish, and give their essays whatever title they choose. The papers must be finished and mailed to Legion headquarters by midnight of June the twenty-first. On July the fifth the awards will be made to the winners at a luncheon in the Coronet Hotel in Rozella." Miss Johnson paused for breath.

"What are the prizes?" demanded a girl named Betty Lou.

"I was about to tell the class, Betty Lou, when you interrupted," sighed Miss Johnson. "The first prize will be a trip to Washington, our nation's capital, with all expenses paid."

The very walls of the schoolroom seemed to breathe in and out, in wonder at the grandeur of such a prize.

"The second prize is fifty dollars in cash," Miss Johnson continued. "The third prize is twenty-five dollars."

"Twenty-five dollars *in cash?*" asked Betty Lou.

"How else, Betty Lou?" Miss Johnson's voice seemed to drop ice cubes down the necks of the 6B's.

In spite of the ice, for the next few seconds every one of the nineteen pupils in the room was enthralled with wonderful visions of mailing a literary masterpiece at the final midnight hour: of honors bestowed: of being well fed at the ritziest hotel in Rozella: of travel: of wealth. But in the cold light of reason, at least sixteen of them soon came to their senses, knowing, as they did, that they were no good at writing essays of any kind.

At home, Little Joe reported the news of the American Legion contest.

"You think you might try, Son?" asked Poppy.

"Who? Me?" asked Little Joe, pointing to himself in alarm. *Shucks!* Poppy would be putting ideas into Mommy's head. A *Pee Wee* who was so busy making home runs at recess: a farmer boy who was working, body and britches, at getting the acreage on its feet: a guy named Joseph Booker Freed, striving toward a passing grade by closing day—*good grief* —trying to write an essay worth anything would be the hardest job of all!

But Mommy walked right up to Little Joe, and laid her hands on his shoulders. She didn't say a word, but her eyes shone into his with a special shining. Her hands on his shoulders had a special pressure, firm and compelling.

The next day Mommy said, quietly, "A boy who could climb the steps of the Lincoln Memorial and stand before Mr. Abraham Lincoln in his big chair —that boy would never forget his trip to Washington, D.C."

SCHOOL AND HOME

The same evening Mommy turned to the word *essay* in the dictionary. *"A thoughtful composition,"* read Mommy. *"To try. To make an effort.* A boy who would try hard to write 'a thoughtful composition' would be a brave boy," Mommy declared. "Even if he didn't win the fifty dollars, or even the twenty-five dollars, to save for his college, he would 've been a brave boy to try."

But Little Joe wasn't ready to say whether he would, or wouldn't try. First, he would have to take time to wrassle with the notion. And he would need to wrassle like sixty!

One day India Rose came home full of starry-eyed excitement. "Mommy!" she cried. "Miss Johnsing says if it's 'greeable to you, she will stop by tomorrow after school."

If Mommy felt fluttery, she didn't let on. "Honey, you tell Miss Johnson it's a very agreeable pleasure."

Pearlie May and India Rose did not go home by bus the next evening. They rode in Miss Johnson's car, on the front seat with her! Little Joe would have enjoyed sharing this honor, but the boys might kid him as "teacher's pet." He rode the bus as usual, arriving home as Mommy was handing out her linen tea napkins with tatting trim. She served tea and delicate home-made cookies in her best china. Poppy wasn't there, as he was helping at Grassy Acres.

Little Joe's cup slid all over his plate when Miss

Johnson said to Mommy, "I am hoping that Joseph Booker will try for one of the Legion's contest prizes."

"Little Joe is wrassling with the notion, Miss Johnson," answered Mommy. *Hm-mm,* how did Mommy know that Little Joe was wrassling? Neither of the women even glanced at him, but for the moment he was the most important person in the room. He squirmed, uneasily. His cup slid around. He dropped a cooky on the floor.

Too, it turned out that Miss Johnson was highly interested in seeing the dictionary. One would have thought it to be the rarest kind of a book—Miss Johnson's tender handling of it—and the proud, admiring way she smiled at Mommy. When Miss Johnson arose to take her leave, she held Mommy's fingers in hers, saying, "I doubt if you realize what it means to me to come into a home where the dictionary is daily reading. You and your children and your dictionary make me wonderfully hopeful and happy."

Then Miss Johnson turned to the children. "Let it be a secret between us," she said, her eyes twinkling, "but I think your mother is my favorite of all my New Hope mothers."

"She's our fav'rit, too," piped Pearlie May.

CHAPTER EIGHT

"Doodah, doodah!"

S o Easter passed. The leaves of the maple grew larger and greener. The lilacs bloomed, and the apple trees. Mr. Carle's bees paid no heed to the ugly sign on the barbed wire fence, but flew over from Golden Grain Farm to gather their loads of honey from the Freed blossoms. May arrived. There were tender new lettuce, scarlet radishes, and crisp onions out of the garden. Mommy planted flower seeds and cuttings where once the old farm-house had stood. Fatty had a litter of piglets. They were like scampering, curly-tailed sausages. "Seems as if baby pigs are made a-purpose to make folks laugh," roared Poppy.

One fine warm Saturday afternoon two families of friends came out from Hoytville. They brought sandwiches, salads and fruits. Mommy made coffee for the grown-ups. Violet furnished milk for the children. Little Joe, India Rose and Pearlie May proudly displayed the baby chicks and pigs, the lamb, and the mysteries of the woodlot. They pointed out the robins' nest in the maple, and the wren box Little Joe had made and fastened to a haw

tree. Mommy showed off her flower and vegetable
gardens. She pulled rosy stalks of rhubarb for her
guests to carry home with them.

Poppy showed his cornplanter and cultivator, his
wagon and plow and harrow. He took the party over
the land. When the far pasture was reached, one of
the boy visitors took instant fire. He picked up a
rock, and threw it angrily at the sign on the fence.
Others picked up clods and stones, meaning to make
a target of the sign and destroy it.

But Poppy held up his hand. "None of that, fellows!" he said. He grinned, making light of it all.
"That sign is Mr. Carle's property. Let it hang.
Not many see it here, 'cept the animals at their graz-
ing, and animals can't read. We don't mind the sign
so much any more, though at first it didn't seem like
Lady Cake. And the children won't ever play here,
though they loved that brook when they first laid
eyes on it. But let the ol' sign hang! Forget it!"

During supper, one of the women asked if the
Freeds had given their farm a name. "Nowadays,
Big Joe," she said, "seems as if it's the style for a
farm to have a fancy name."

"Yeah," agreed Poppy. "There's Grassy Acres on
one side of us, and Golden Grain Farm on 't other.
Over near New Hope School there's New Hope
Farm. But we'll wait 'til ours grows into a paying
venture 'fore we name it. Even then, it might be
thought too uppity of us, to set up a name-board

out front. Prob'ly we'll name it private among us, and just for the fun of it."

However, the Freeds and their guests had a jolly time suggesting names for the farm. *"Ramshackle-Barn Place* would tie right in," joked Poppy. His daughters were horrified. "We should have a pretty name for our pretty farm!" cried India Rose. She ran for her book, *I Love Poetry.* Turning the pages, words and phrases popped up at India Rose. *"Bob-White Acres* would be nice," she announced. The poetry in India Rose fairly boiled over. *"Morning Dew Farm*—that would be lovely!" she declared, recklessly.

Little Joe suggested *Big Maple Farm.* Mommy said, "We could call it *Bittersweet Farm."* She smiled at her children, and they smiled back, the dictionary secret warm between them. Pearlie May, who had been racking her brain, then said she would like to name the place *Fairy Belle Farm,* after the song by Stephen Foster.

> "She sings to the meadows and she carols
>   to the streams,
> She laughs in the sunlight and smiles
>   while in her dreams."

sang Pearlie May, remembering the meadow, the brook, and the sunlight on *her* farm.

The boys all but snorted at such a fancy suggestion. But Pearlie May's music made everyone, young and old, eager to sing. They hurried to pack away the supper things. They put on their wraps and gathered under the big maple. Its leaves glistened in the moonlight.

Oh, it was good, singing together in the May moonshine! They sang hymns, and spirituals. They sang sentimental old songs which give all but frogs, snakes and rhinoceroses the most delightful heartaches.

"The days go by like a shadow o'er the heart," crooned the singers, knowing that it was sometimes true, yet believing, for the moment, not a word of it. . . . "Way down upon the Swanee ribber, Far, far away." Soprano, alto, tenor blended. *Far, far away* echoed silver-toned from the silvery meadows and the white moonlit roadways.

Pearlie May soloed, flinging capers while her friends clapped the time. "I win my money on de bobtail nag, Doodah, doodah!" And the chorus rolled out, merry with many voices, "Oh, doodah-day!"

Alone, Pearlie May sang other songs, old and new. If, after that, Mister Robin's solos were more tuneful, no doubt it was because he had listened from the maple tree to Pearlie May Freed.

So at last the guests departed, whole-hearted and light-hearted with melody. "Doodah, doodah!"

Mr. Cummings dropped by the next evening. "Wife pretty nearly went into a swoon last night,

listening to your music. She made us keep all the doors and windows open, so she wouldn't miss a note. 'Prettiest singing I ever heard!' Wife declared. 'I could sit and listen all night and every night!'

"But I think I must tell you, Big Joe," Mr. Cummings went on. "Mort Carle almost went into a swoon, too. Worse! He went so far as to telephone the sheriff. Ordered him to come out and arrest the lot of you for disturbing the peace!"

Mommy sank into the nearest chair and fanned herself with her apron. Poppy gave a snort. "I don't see how a string of harmless songs that everybody sings, can disturb the peace. And come to think of it, by the time the sound traveled across Carle's acres, it would 've been shushed down to a pretty faint harkening. Mort Carle just used our singing as an excuse to give his spitework the go sign!" Poppy was upset.

"Hush, Big Joe!" Mommy chided him. "Let's reason, fair-minded, if we might 've been disturbing the peace without knowing it." Mommy turned to Mr. Cummings. "Why didn't the sheriff come, then, and arrest us?" she asked.

Jim Cummings chuckled. "Well, the sheriff did speed out here, at about seventy per. But when he got within clear hearing, he pulled up and listened. Then the music took hold of him. Yes, sir, his Nibs the Sheriff just sat there enjoying himself. Finally he came to my place, and found us hanging spellbound out of the windows. 'D'you just naturally hate that pretty harmonizin', Mr. and Mrs. Cummings?' he asked us. 'Does it disturb your peace?'

"My wife answered the sheriff. 'If that's disturbing the peace,' she declared, 'then I'd like my peace disturbed often. Why, it's just the opposite,' Wife said. 'It brings peace. It does my soul good—that sweet music wafting through the moonlit air!'

"So the sheriff waited until your sing-fest was over, mourning that he hadn't brought his wife, so she could hear it also. Then Sheriff made the excuse it might be too late to call on Mort Carle. But he 'phoned me today and said Carle called him early this morning, asking if he'd made the arrest. To make a long story short," related Mr. Cummings, "Carle was so hot he 'most set the telephone a-fire when Sheriff told him he'd found the other neighbors enjoying the music, and that he himself had considered it mighty soothing. That's the end of the story, as far as it goes," said Mr. Cummings. He took a laughing leave.

Mommy couldn't laugh much. She was troubled. *As far as it goes*—she couldn't help remembering those words.

But Poppy pranced out to do the evening milking, shouting "Doodah! doodah!" Little Joe and the girls followed, beating on the milk pails and the chicken-feed pan, singing, "Oh! doodah-day!"

CHAPTER NINE

The New Dresses

On the school bus Monday morning Judy Cummings inquired eagerly of India Rose how soon the Freeds were going to have another singing party. India Rose and Pearlie May, who always sat together in the bus, were struck tongue-tied when Mirzda Dorbe joined in and said what she did.

"My mother and I have nice time Saturday night hearing music. In my country we sing like that, my mother say, in much crowds of people," said Mirzda.

India Rose collected her wits, quickly. "It's nice you liked the singing, Mirzda," she said. "But Mr. Carle didn't like it," she added, with sudden spunk.

"Na!" agreed Mirzda. "But Mrs. Carle, she like! Okay she like. My mother she tell, ya!" Mirzda lifted her hand to her mouth and hissed from behind it, to show how Mrs. Carle had secretly confided in Mirzda's mother. India Rose and Pearlie May didn't know how they could wait until evening to tell Mommy and Poppy and Little Joe this startling piece of news, and that Mirzda herself seemed more friendly.

"It's a pleasure to know that one and all at Golden Grain Farm are not lined up against us," said Mommy.

"Don't count too much on it," advised Poppy. "Let's try to forget the whole thing. We've got other matters to study on." He and Little Joe, as partners, fell to discussing the corn-planting which should be done by mid-May, the weather allowing. Little Joe complained that school held on too late in the season. "It's all right for boys on farms where they own tractors. But with us, the plowing and planting will take a lot longer. If I could only stay at home and help you, Poppy!" grumbled Little Joe.

However, the end of school was within sight, although it would come too late for the corn-planting. It had been a week ago, at the end of April, that Miss Johnson had called the pupils together in the gymnasium. She said, "About four weeks of school remain before the summer vacation." She waited while the children bounced and beamed. Then she went on. "As usual, we shall have some nice closing-day exercises, with your parents as guests. This morning we shall hold our first chorus practice." Miss Johnson smiled over at the piano, as if it were an obliging friend. "Everyone will be in the chorus, big and little. There is a solo part, which is to be given to Pearlie May Freed."

Pearlie May fluttered like a butterfly on a pin.

THE NEW DRESSES

All the same, she was proud!

"I have selected an interesting patriotic play, with parts for five pupils. In this play, Mirzda Dorbe is to take the part of a brand-new American," explained Miss Johnson.

Mirzda's pink cheeks grew scarlet. Her long flaxen braids bobbled. She smiled at everyone, her eyes very blue.

Miss Johnson read the names of those who would speak recitations. India Rose was on the list.

Besides singing in the chorus, Little Joe was to help decorate the gymnasium with flowers and green branches. He was to help tack up the best art work, and the neatest, most perfect papers in spelling, arithmetic and composition, to show the parents.

After school that day the Freed children leaped from the bus and flew into the house to tell what was expected of them on Closing Day. Mommy's dark eyes shone. "For Miss Johnson and your teachers, for the children and their parents, our Pearlie May will sing like a bird in a tree," she said. "Our Indy Rose will outfavor herself when she speaks her piece. And Miss Johnson never saw a boy who can fix up a gym as fancy-fine as Joseph Booker Freed." Mommy searched for the word *decorate* in the dictionary. *"To ornament: adorn,"* quoted Mommy, with delight.

The next day she said, "I've been thinking it

would be proper for Little Joe to ornament himself with a new shirt, the last day of school. Indy Rose and Pearlie May might be adorned in new dresses."

"Can't afford new clothes," muttered Little Joe, with a wise, old-man air. "We been buying seeds and plants and fertilizer 'n' everything. We got High-Stepper and Levi and Vi'let to store-feed 'til we grow our own hay and corn."

"If Little Joe thinks he can make do without a new shirt, let him make do," said Poppy, patting his son on the head. "But so the girls have new dresses, we'll work a little harder and stretch a little farther."

"We'll jus' toil and moil, Poppy!" promised India Rose and Pearlie May, sizzling excitedly.

The next Friday (it was the day before the singing party) Mrs. Sargent came after Mommy, as usual, to do the weekly cleaning. While she was away, and after school was dismissed, Little Joe and the girls weeded the garden patch. India Rose, weeding with might and main, practiced saying her recitation. Pearlie May, toiling and moiling, practiced her solo part.

"Sounds mighty fetching, Indy Rose." Little Joe praised his sister. "Sounds like a bird in a tree, Pearlie May."

"Pretty soon Mommy will be home with our new dresses," trilled the girls.

THE NEW DRESSES

They could scarcely wait for Mommy to untie the package, when at last she returned. "I found us some bargains," announced Mommy, beaming. "These dresses have good, sound seams. They're color-fast. They were marked down only because they are a teeny-weeny shop-soiled. But a little clean store dirt don't harm them. I'll do them up my prettiest."

"Mommy, the dresses are so beautiful they dizzy us!" cried the girls. One dress was pink-and-green check. The other was blue-and-green. Each had a tucked white yoke, edged all around with a ruffle. Poppy and Little Joe pronounced them "classy."

"Will you souse them in the Monday wash, Mommy?" asked Pearlie May.

"No, these pretty dresses I'll wash and iron to themselves on a Saturday, when you are home to help with the other work. A week from tomorrow I'll do up the dresses. Then I'll hang them away, finicky and fine, until Closing Day at school."

India Rose ran to mark the day on the calendar. While they were at it, they marked Closing Day.

The Saturday rolled around. The sun shone brightly, ready to do its part in drying the dresses. "Those baby clouds up there in the sky are jus' playing with their toes," giggled Pearlie May. While the sun shone and the clouds played, Pearlie May washed the dishes. India Rose swept and dusted the rooms. They worked busily at many chores, so that Mommy could devote all her care to laundering the new frocks. At last Mommy hung them on the clothes line out of doors.

Then she and the girls went over the rise to hoe and weed the potato patch. "We feel dancy and prancy," sang the girls. They cut comical dingdoes as they looked back to see their new dresses drying in the sun. Below them, Poppy and Little Joe were plowing the ten-acre field. It didn't really matter that they were too far away to hear India Rose and Pearlie May yelling, "Hi, Poppy! Hi, Little Joe! We feel twirty and flirty!"

Nothing mattered much just now, except those dapper twin dresses flirting on the line.

CHAPTER TEN

The Cyclone

As every gardener knows, weeds are tricky things. They even play tricks on such good, hard-working little girls as India Rose and Pearlie May Freed. That Saturday morning, the sisters discovered that where there was but one weed to dig out, two weeds seemed to take its place, with roots as deep and stubborn as roots can be. So that's the slow and weary way it went with them, row by row in the potato patch. Before long, in spite of being so happy about their new dresses, the girls were feeling anything but twirty and flirty.

But they kept on, so busy they scarcely noticed how the baby morning clouds had grown into big dark fellows, swaggering and fuming all over the sky. Suddenly a warning rush of wind swept across the land. Mommy and the children lifted their eyes to see Poppy waving at them. "Storm coming!" shouted Poppy. "Run to the house!"

They saw Poppy unhitching Levi, leaving the plow in the furrow. They saw Poppy remove Levi's harness. There was no time to drive Levi to shelter in the barn, where High-Stepper was now taking things easy. *Pooh,* any creature as tough as a mule could surely withstand a spring thunderstorm. While Little Joe, laughing, raced against the wind, Poppy, with the harness over his arm, bounded over the rise and caught up with his hurrying family. As they dashed across the house yard, Poppy swept up the lamb, which had been daintily nibbling grass.

"Listen!" Little Joe stopped short. "Sounds like a big streamliner coming this way, or an airplane, full speed."

"It's no train or plane!" Poppy yelled. "It's wind, and a whopper! Hurry!" He all but stumbled over Cinderella, mewing and scratching at the kitchen door. She streaked in as Poppy opened it.

He and Little Joe had to exert all their strength to close that door against the gale. Mommy rushed around to see that no windows were open. Above the roar of rain and wind, she cried, "Get to the cellar!" She snatched the precious dictionary, precious Abraham Lincoln. She and Poppy followed the children down the steps.

In the cellar the lamb looked forlorn and out of place. Cinderella crouched in a corner, her eyes gleaming like small headlights. Poppy and Mommy, the children, the dictionary, the Lincoln photograph, the lamb and the cat—in the cellar—and the world filled with the great clamor of the storm! The lightning crackled, the thunder crashed, the rain poured down, but these separate sounds were lost in the boom and roar of the wind.

India Rose clutched at Mommy's arm. She wailed in Mommy's ear. "Our dresses! What will happen to our dresses?"

"Oh, Mommy, we forgot to bring in the dresses!" sobbed Pearlie May.

Mommy shook her head and mouthed her words. They had to read her lips. "There was no time to get the dresses. I'm thinking of our maple tree. God save our dear, noble tree!"

It seemed to the family in the cellar that the storm roared above their heads for a long time. Actually it whirled away within a few ear-splitting moments. Poppy leaped up the steps two at a time. The others, including Cinderella, scrambled up. They made for the open kitchen door, where Poppy now stood, gazing out in silence. They could tell, by the look of Poppy's back, that he was too astonished to speak.

The others, crowding close, could only stare and gasp. It was the barn which made them gasp. It was no longer the shape or the size of a barn. It was not a barn at all. It was a mass of fallen timbers. A little beyond its topsy-turvy tumble, the roof lay spread out, still holding its shape. And atop the roof, standing on his four big, hairy feet, was High-

Stepper the horse. High-Stepper's head drooped, as if in shame at the trick the wind had played on him. But he was unharmed. Even though the barn was a hopeless wreck, and no telling what the Freeds would do without it, or when and how they would get a new barn, High-Stepper was such a funny sight that Poppy and the children burst out laughing.

But no one laughed for long. What else had happened? Were the pigs and chickens blown into slivers of tails, scraps of feathers? Was Violet safe in the far pasture? Was Levi the mule all of a piece? Were the other buildings standing? What about the trees?

The hearts of the Freeds lifted up when they saw the maple. The earth beneath was covered with wet leaves, but the tree itself stood as staunch and straight as ever. In the lane one of the locusts was riven from top to bottom, its broken boughs sweeping the ground. Another had been snapped off at about Little Joe's height, leaving only a pitiful stump. The locust trees and the barn had been in the direct path of the wind. The corn crib, too, was partly wrecked. Some of the trees in the woodlot had lost a few branches. But the chickens and the pigs were unharmed. The garage stood shipshape.

Poppy led High-Stepper gingerly off the fallen roof. Then he and Little Joe hastened to the ten-

acre field to see about Levi. The mule was mud to his knees. Even his ears were mud-spattered from the newly turned furrows. He was switching his tail, angrily. Otherwise, he seemed the same Levi. Doubtless, the things that Levi might have said, had he the gift of speech, would not have been fit for gentle ears. How in blazes was a mule to eat, without his old manger? Where in thunder was a mule to sleep, without his comfortable stall? Not even a roof over the head of a hard-working, earn-as-you-go mule!

Little Joe found Violet lying down in the far pasture. It had been the most sensible thing she could have done, under the blasts of the storm. When she was brought back to the site of her old shelter, she just went on chewing her cud. It was business as usual with Violet. Violet had a lot of poise.

Little Joe said, "When I was down at the far end, I thought maybe I'd find Mr. Carle's sign carried off by the wind. But it's there, same as ever."

Poppy let out his breath, wearily. "That sign is the least of our troubles just now. Reckon that was a real-for-sure cyclone, but lands' sakes, we have so much to be thankful for!"

"Just don't we!" exclaimed Mommy. "Ourselves. Our house. Our tree. Our animals."

India Rose and Pearlie May didn't like to spoil this fine spirit of thankfulness in their parents. But

—hadn't they run here, there, and everywhere, searching frantically for their dresses? Not a shred of the pretty new frocks was to be found, not a button! The girls were heartbroken. They couldn't keep from crying. Rather loudly, too.

"Now, hush, my dearies," said Mommy, bravely. "On the last day of school Pearlie May will wear her old dress. But Pearlie May will sing like a bird in a tree. Indy Rose will wear her old dress. But Indy Rose will out-favor herself, speaking her piece."

"Same as me, in my old shirt," Little Joe reminded his sisters. "Guess I can fancy up the gym and sing in the chorus without a new shirt."

Such remarks were small comfort to the two little mourners. The loss of their new dresses was a sorrow-laden thing.

However, the girls were trying their bravest to bear up, when Mirzda Dorbe ran fleetly into the yard. Mirzda's cheeks, usually so rosy, were pale. Her breath came fast. She had run a long way. She stopped before Poppy and looked up at him.

"You are to quick come," Mirzda gasped. "Mr. Carle has high fall from barn. Today he is painting barn from ladder and buckets of paint. He is stubber like mule when Mrs. Carle scold that storm come soon. Mr. Carle say, 'Okay, Wife, drops of rain is not hurting me. I will paint a two shakes

THE CYCLONE

longer.' But then the wind fly. The ladder is shaking and falling. Mr. Carle is falling, falling. Does he speak? Na! Does he live? We not know!"

"But where is your father, and Mr. Carle's son, that they cannot help?" asked Poppy.

"All day my father and Bob Carle go in truck to Rozella," answered Mirzda. "They buy cattle in Rozella. When storm come they not home. Na! Mr. Carle is lying too heavy for Mrs. Carle and my mother. They cannot lift. The telephone is knock out. Mrs. Carle cannot leave the mister and fly for help. She say Big Joe Freed is strongest and nearby neighbor. 'Run quick,' she is saying to me."

Poppy looked at Mommy. "Now that they need help, the Carles call me *neighbor*," he said bitterly.

"*Neighbor* is a strong and friendly word," answered Mommy. "Go, Big Joe Freed. Go quickly," Mommy said. "Take Little Joe with you. Perhaps Little Joe can help."

Poppy ran for his bike. He streaked off up the road toward Golden Grain Farm.

Little Joe rushed down cellar and struggled up again with the lamb. Everyone else had forgotten it. Then he and Mirzda set off together. A little distance up the road they climbed a fence and took a short cut across the wet fields.

CHAPTER ELEVEN

Surprises

Little Joe lay on his back under the big maple. *Boy,* it was good to spread out flat and do nothing this Sunday afternoon! Mommy had said, "Everyone of us should rest, after such a hard week." She herself was in the house, dozing in her chair, but keeping watch over tired Poppy, who slept soundly on the day bed.

But were India Rose and Pearlie May resting? Of course not! They were off again with Judy Cummings and Mirzda Dorbe, on another thorough search for their lost dresses. Seemed as if those girls never would give up hope.

If they found the dresses it would need to be soon. The coming Friday was Closing Day at school. And was Little Joe glad! He raised his head a lazy two inches and sniffed the good smell of new lumber. The planks, allowed Poppy at cost by Tom Sargent, were piled high, ready for the building of a new barn, beginning tomorrow. The concrete posts for the frame were already up. The litter and mess of the old barn had been cleared away, although it was only a week ago that the cyclone had wrecked it. Neighbors had helped to clear up the fallen timbers, the fallen trees—the Freeds' *own* neighbors—Jim Cummings, young Bob Carle, and Antons Dorbe, Mirzda's father. Last Thursday Antons had been sent with the Golden Grain Farm tractor and corn planter, the very latest in models. It would have taken Poppy about five days to plant ten acres in corn, his way. With the tractor and corn planter, Antons Dorbe had done it in a day. The neighbors were going to help raise the barn. Bad neighbors could become wonderfully kind and helpful, thought Little Joe, although it took a cyclone to work the change.

"This is the life!" thought Little Joe, enjoying a stretch and a yawn. "All over America there are people living on farms. Big and little farms, the people working hard, but surely, pretty happy, like us Freeds. Even if a person must live in a city, living in America is wonderful. 'Specially," thought Little Joe, "is it wonderful for a girl like Mirzda Dorbe.

"But, hold on! Isn't it quite as wonderful for a boy like Joseph Booker Freed?" he mused. "If ever I could 've talked with Abraham Lincoln, there in his temple in Washington, D.C., I could 've told him it is wonderful, for me, and for Mirzda, and for everybody. He would 've liked hearing that, I bet, a great American like Abe Lincoln."

Washington, D.C.! Little Joe turned over, uneasily. *It was tough, the way he was still wrassling with the notion of entering the American Legion contest. It was like being obliged to wrassle, day after day, with a kid that's bigger, who gets you down and sits on you, more often than not. Only about three weeks left, now, to write that essay, in case he decided to do it. If only Mommy and Poppy and Miss Johnson did not expect such a hard task of a boy who would rather just jog along, working and playing, farmer boy-like, now that summer vacation was at hand! Wonder what Abraham Lincoln would tell a boy to do—a Negro boy who might climb the steps of the temple and stand before Abe and ask his advice.*

Well! Little Joe did another restless flop. *Well, it's pretty certain Abe would caution that boy to go ahead and tackle that essay. Bet Mr. Abraham Lincoln would be kind, like always, and tell Joseph Booker Freed a few fine, prize-winning things to say in his essay.*

Little Joe raised his head. Here came those girls. He was glad to see them. Their chatter quickly dispelled the boy's visions of Abraham Lincoln. "Find your dresses?" he asked, lazily teasing.

"Joe Freed!" cried India Rose. "D'you think if we'd found our dresses we'd be standing here just like ordinary every day?"

The girls were barefoot. Their shoes, fastened to-

gether in pairs, were slung over their arms. The edges of their skirts were wet. "We been wading in our own pretty brook," explained Pearlie May.

The girls flung themselves down on the grass under the tree. "Tell me 'bout Mr. Carle and the cyclone 'n' everything, Joe," urged Judy. "The cyclone missed Grassy Acres, and it so close, too!" Judy complained.

Little Joe grinned. "I've told you once. Bet Mirzda's told you a dozen times."

"I can't always get things straight when Mirzda talks," Judy said. " 'Scuse me, Mirzda. I couldn't do half as well if I tried to talk your language, I know."

Mirzda, encouraged by Judy's praise, checked Mr. Carle's injuries off on her fingers. "Mr. Carle is lying in hospital in Rozella," she said. "He has much hurt. He has broke leg. He has broke toe. He has broke bone to his collar. He has crack in his head."

The children couldn't help laughing.

"Mr. Carle is in hospital long time," Mirzda went on, still more heartened by her friends' merriment. "But when he is coming home again, he comes home vell. Okay, the doctor makes promise to Mrs. Carle, ya!"

"Now you tell, Joe," begged Judy.

But Mirzda had not finished. That big wind was unforgettable. "The cyclone a prize cow killed at

Golden Grain Farm," she related. "The cyclone a few trees knock over. But the big danger the cyclone made on Mr. Carle and ladder."

Judy made frantic signs to Little Joe behind Mirzda's back. He took the hint. "That day," he began, "there was Mr. Carle lying like dead by the barn. *Man,* he was a sight! Besides being sopping wet with rain, he was all over red paint. Poppy had to cut some of his clothes off him, where they were stiff with paint. Poppy rigged up a stretcher with a half-size mattress, some leather straps and a blanket. I helped, but I don't know enough, and I'm not big enough to help much," admitted Little Joe. "The women and Mirzda and I helped to get Mr. Carle on the stretcher and into the house. The telephone wasn't working, so Poppy drove the station wagon into Hoytville. I went along. On the way we saw lots of things the cyclone had done. Even in Hoytville trees were down. Poppy and I went to the doctor's office. He promised to go to Golden Grain Farm right away. Poppy and I went to tell Mr. Sargent 'bout the cyclone on our place. Then we drove back. The doctor said Mr. Carle would live all right. So we didn't wait for the ambulance from Rozella, nor for Bob Carle and Mirzda's father to come home. That's about all," finished Little Joe.

He didn't tell how much he had admired the fine big barn at Golden Grain Farm, nor the farm shop, fitted up with everything modern that heart could wish. For Little Joe had taken a hasty peep at the buildings. The big poultry house and the hog sheds —*well,* Mr. Carle's hens and hogs certainly had it soft! Neither would Little Joe admit to Mirzda and Judy how ritzy he had felt, riding into Hoytville in the station wagon, with the name, *Golden Grain Farm,* printed prosperously on the sides.

But now, India Rose took up the tale. "Judy, the day after the cyclone—it was last Sunday afternoon —Mr. Bob Carle came here. He took his wallet out of his pocket. He said, 'We 'presh'ate the help you gave my father yesterday, Big Joe Freed. I would like to pay you something in return for the favor.' "

At this point, Pearlie May jumped to her feet, the better to act out the next episode. She drew herself up, proudly. "Our poppy made himself straight!" cried Pearlie May. "He said, 'Mr. Bob, if one of your other neighbors had done your father the favor, you wouldn't be offering him money. In your eyes I may be different, Mr. Bob Carle. All the same, I take no money for helping a neighbor.'

"So Mr. Bob put away his wallet, and he turned red a-doing of it," Pearlie May continued. "Then Mr. Bob asked my poppy, 'What can I do to show my 'presh'ation?' "

Pearlie May stopped, very suddenly, and sat down. She had seen Little Joe and India Rose telling her with their eyes to stop. After a moment India Rose said, "So Mr. Bob Carle had our corn-planting done, and he says he will help build the barn. Poppy didn't ask it, but of course it's nice."

So the Freed children hadn't told all. There were some things they didn't care to talk about, and the sign on the fence was one of them. But they remembered, vividly, the answer Poppy had given Bob Carle as to what could be done in the way of appreciation.

Poppy had answered, "Mr. Bob, for the sake of my children, could you Carles manage to get along without the sign on your fence you put up to tell us, as ugly as possible, that we weren't welcome in these parts? D'you think it would hurt you any to take that sign down?"

"I took that sign down exactly one hour ago," Mr. Bob had declared. "When I was at the hospital this morning, and told Dad of the happenings yesterday, he ordered me to remove the sign first chance I got. My dad said, 'Guess I was a little hasty hot, putting up that sign against neighbors.' "

"Thanks," Big Joe had answered Bob Carle. "Now my children can play in their own brook, the way children ought to play, free and happy."

Under the maple tree, the Freed children knew how free and happy they were feeling, with that sign gone. Now they could really enjoy their new life on the farm. India Rose fell back on the grass, her head on her arms. Half dreaming, she began to recite the lines of her Closing Day recitation. And suddenly, surprisingly—*plop!*—an old rag of a thing fell out of the maple tree, right across India Rose's knees.

She squealed and jumped to her feet. She snatched up the rag and shook it out. It was one of the checkered dresses! It was India Rose's dress, the blue-and-green one!

The children went wild. Mommy came hurrying to the door, trying to shush them. But she couldn't make herself heard above the shouts and laughter. The children couldn't stop dancing and cavorting. And when Mommy saw what had really happened, a woman three times her size could not have shown more astonishment. "It's pure wonderment!" she cried. "This dress looks like a rag, but all it needs is soap and water, starch and a hot iron!" Laughing, Mommy called for Poppy.

"Swanny!" roared Poppy, when he had staggered out and rubbed the sleep from his eyes. "That ol' cyclone played a lot of freakish tricks, but this trick is the freakiest!"

"Maybe—" muttered Little Joe. All at once he was climbing the tree, his bare feet finding toe-hold on the trunk. Up shinned Little Joe from branch to branch, while the others watched, breathlessly.

At last he hooked one leg over a bough. He began unwinding something plastered against the trunk, away up there. Little Joe, calling out to Pearlie May, dropped the object into her eager, outstretched arms. It was Pearlie May's pink-and-green checked frock!

When Mommy could pry the dress out of her daughter's tight, happy grip, she smoothed it out. "The ruffle is ripped away in one place," announced Mommy. "The white yoke is a mite stained." And once Little Joe was safely down out of the tree, Mommy sewed the ruffle on again. She took out the brown stain with bleaching powder.

The next afternoon, when the sisters returned from school, Mommy said, "Tickle-toe to the clothes-press, and peep in." Giggling, India Rose and Pearlie May tickle-toed. They peeped. There hung the new frocks, washed, starched, and ironed, as fine and finicky as if hanging in a stylish dress shop. That night it seemed to the girls there had never been so many stars sparkling amid the branches of the maple tree. "Thank you, our tree," whispered India Rose and Pearlie May, "for keeping our dresses safe and sound when the cyclone blew them right into your arms."

When Closing Day came, the gymnasium of New Hope School was beautiful. Other boys had run hither and yon to bring flowers and green boughs.

SURPRISES

But Little Joe Freed had run fastest and farthest. Little Joe's help in arranging exhibits for the parents was a neat job. When Little Joe sang in the chorus, no one noticed that he wore his old shirt, because it was so spankin' clean, and the lad's face so bright.

Pearlie May sang as sweet and flute-y as a bird in a tree. When India Rose spoke her recitation, she outfavored herself so much that even she could scarcely believe her ears. But no wonder! The sisters were wearing their pert new frocks. "These are our cyclone dresses," explained India Rose and Pearlie May to anyone kind enough to compliment them.

Good-byes were spoken to schoolmates and teachers. Miss Johnson told Little Joe, "If you need me for anything special within the next month, Joseph, I shall be at my home in Hoytville."

Answered Little Joe, "I might need you special, Miss Johnsing. Any minute now I'm going to begin wrassling with my essay for the Legion contest." Deciding like that, suddenly and certainly, rather surprised Little Joe himself.

Mommy said nothing until evening. "I won't ask you what you plan to say, Little Joe, nor how you aim to write it out. But God give you the power and grace to say it."

"And Abraham Lincoln," answered Little Joe.

"Mommy, I'm playin' like I'm standing in that temple." The boy pointed to the photograph of the Lincoln Memorial. "In my essay I'm talking to Abe about America, there in his big chair."

"That's a true-hearted fancy that's taken hold of you, Son," Mommy said. "See the words on the temple wall above Abraham Lincoln's head. . . . *in the hearts of the people . . . his memory . . . enshrined forever*. But Son, we of the dark skins were Abe's special sad and heavy burden. We are Abe's children, forever. If you'll listen, careful, Abraham Lincoln will tell you what to say. So don't you go to doing all the talking, and tell Abe what America owes you. Listen close. Abraham Lincoln will tell Little Joe Freed what he owes America."

CHAPTER TWELVE

In Rozella

Poppy, India Rose, and Pearlie May sat in the back seat. Mommy and Little Joe rode in the front. Miss Johnson drove. It was her car. She was taking the Freeds the twenty-five miles to Rozella. It was the fifth of July, a hot, bright day. The Freeds had done some tall hustling that morning, getting the chores done, taking their baths, one by one, getting dressed in their best. India Rose and Pearlie May were wearing their cyclone dresses. Mommy wore a new hat, very neat and becoming. Poppy declared he felt like a stuffed toad, wearing a coat after working bare-armed for the past month. Little Joe had on brand-new slacks and shirt. "You lend me the money for the duds, Poppy," Little Joe had said. "I'll pay you back."

"Okay, Son," agreed Poppy.

It had taken eleven dollars to fit himself out, counting his new shoes, and all. Eleven dollars from fifty, and he would have thirty-nine dollars left. *Clothes*—they were a nuisance! But of course it was highly necessary, this time, for Little Joe to be well dressed.

LADYCAKE FARM

For Joseph Booker Freed had won second prize in the American Legion contest. This morning he was on his way to Rozella and the Coronet Hotel to receive it. He felt pretty rich. He also felt quite scared—a happy, thrilled scaredness.

Poppy and Miss Johnson seemed to be the only ones who were able to talk. Miss Johnson drove the car at a fast clip, but flung her words expertly over her shoulder to Poppy. He leaned forward, tossing his words over to Miss Johnson.

"Fields look mighty good this year," observed Farmer Poppy. . . . "Doesn't that new-mown hay smell divine?" raved Miss Johnson. . . . "Soon as I get the farm really running," confided Poppy, "I'm going to disk in a lot of commercial fertilizer and seed my fields with forage. I'm going in for beef cattle. My farm's too small to expect to make anything with crops only.". . . "Take my advice and have two or three acres in truck crops," said Miss Johnson. She laughed, gaily. "I was raised on a farm. I'm a farm gal."

India Rose and Pearlie May were behaving like deaf and dumb girls. They were still half-stunned by the turn of events. Such pride as they felt in Little Joe! Such high hopes they had of this day! However, they were bursting with a secret. Every two minutes they would clap their hands over their mouths. They acted downright silly. But their dancing eyes and giggles added to the general excitement.

No one else knew the secret except Mommy, but she sat so quietly she might almost not have been there. Except for her hand on Little Joe's hand, giving him strength and courage.

Little Joe had nothing to say, either. He was drained empty of words. Oh, how he had wrassled with words for his essay! He had chewed his pencil to crumbs. He had dug holes in his paper pad. He had scratched his head and groaned aloud. Mommy had fed him on nectar-and-honey, or at least on lots of milk and bacon and greens and bread and butter. His sisters had tiptoed about, believing if they could manage to keep perfectly quiet, the words of Brother's essay would blossom on his paper as richly as the cockscomb bloomed in Mommy's flower garden. But like a poor old miner who digs at hard-pan, Brother had needed to drive at the dictionary, until at last he struck pay-dirt. Then, just in time, Mommy would come to help him dig out the precious nugget—the golden word, the *right* word.

But through it all, Abraham Lincoln had kept Little Joe going. He knew that it was Abraham who had told him, again and again, what American citizenship should mean to an eleven-year-old boy. At last, when the essay was in fair shape, Miss Johnson had looked it over. And she forgot to act like a schoolteacher. She forgot to call the boy *Joseph Booker*. "Joe! My dear Joe!" she caroled. "Your idea is wonderful, and the talk between the imaginary Negro boy and Abraham Lincoln is splendid! This is your work—your very own! But we'll polish off the rough corners, you and I. Oh, I feel certain that this essay, *A Talk with Abraham Lincoln,* will win that first-prize trip to Washington!"

But it had not. When the news came, Miss Johnson had given the judges a tongue-lashing, although not within miles of them. "Year after year and forevermore," cried Miss Johnson, extravagantly, "judges of contests never fail to miss the boat when it comes to awarding first prize!"

"I'd just about as lief have the fifty dollars as the trip," grinned Little Joe, trying to comfort everyone, including himself.

"The second prize is wonderful," said Mommy, "and we are just the same proud of Little Joe. Some other day he will go to Washington. He will say 'howdy-do' to Abraham Lincoln. He will say 'thank-you' to Abraham, for himself, and for all boys and girls."

"It will be a once-upon-a-time wonder story come true, when Little Joe goes to Washington," declared Pearlie May.

"He will go to Washington if I have to take him myself," announced Miss Johnson. Her eyes glittered, as if she had made up her mind, then and there, the date, the hour, and the minute when she and Joseph Booker Freed would take off for Washington.

Poppy soothed them all. "Remember," he said, "there was only one second prize. And it's Lady Cake, the very finest Lady Cake, that out of the whole state our Little Joe won it."

Lady Cake, again! When Poppy said that, a bright idea had popped into the minds of India Rose and Pearlie May. At the very same instant, too. So it had become a jolly little secret, shared with Mommy. It was a private family affair, and it must wait at home. For now, on the morning of the fifth, Miss Johnson and the Freeds were entering the city of Rozella.

"Shall I drop you at the hotel, while I find a parking place?" asked Miss Johnson.

"We'd best keep together," Poppy answered. For how could the family do without Miss Johnson, their guardian angel?

There were only two blocks to walk back from the parking place. The Freeds were glad to stretch their legs and become used to being in Rozella. Here was the Coronet Hotel, the ritziest in town, looming up before them. It overlooked City Park, a green square with benches, a fountain, and graveled paths. Directly opposite, across the park, stood Rozella Manor, the second ritziest hotel.

Briskly, Miss Johnson led her party right up to the Coronet's entrance. A door man stepped forward, bowing. "Will you kindly wait a moment?" He entered the revolving door, beckoning to a gentleman inside the hotel. This gentleman hurried out. Drawing Miss Johnson aside, he spoke to her in low tones.

"Brace yourself," Poppy murmured to Mommy. "Something's happened, and I know what 't is as well as I know my own name."

Miss Johnson joined her companions. "Come," she said. She led them into the park, motioning them to a vacant bench.

"Miss Johnson, please don't tell Little Joe," they heard Poppy whisper.

But Mommy spoke up, clearly. "Little Joe is big enough to write a patriotic essay that won second prize. He is big enough to hear what has happened, and big enough not to mind. We are all big enough," declared Mommy.

"Do we have to go back home?" asked Pearlie May. Her mouth trembled.

"Certainly not," answered Miss Johnson. "Everything will be quite all right. Little Joe will collect his prize, the same as planned. But I see I must tell you," Miss Johnson explained, "and I'll say it right out. When the people who run the Coronet Hotel heard yesterday that our Joseph is a contest winner they said, 'It is against the policy of this hotel to entertain colored people. Therefore we cannot hold the Legion luncheon here.'"

Five dark faces lengthened. The wonder and brightness of the day dimmed. Had it been worth while, then, for Little Joe Freed to win a prize?

"But never mind. Do cheer up!" cried Miss Johnson, hastily. "The luncheon is to be held yonder in the Rozella Manor. I always did like it better than the Coronet. You will like it, too. Everything will be lovely! Everyone will be there, just the same, the Legionnaires, the prize winners, and all the guests. You don't need to mind a bit. Please!" urged Miss Johnson, coaxing smiles from the Freeds. "Now come, or we shall be late," she went on, and then she laughed. "Joseph Booker Freed, enjoy yourself!" she commanded. "All of you Freeds, enjoy yourselves! This is a bright occasion!"

The tight bands of worry and sorrow loosened the hearts of the Freeds. After all, the sun was shining gloriously! After all, their Little Joe had won a fine prize! They walked across the park to Rozella Manor.

CHAPTER THIRTEEN

Lady Cake, Again

Rozella Manor was quite ritzy enough. One minute the feet of Little Joe, India Rose and Pearlie May would be slip-sliding on marble. The next minute they would be sinking into velvety carpet pile so thick it was like walking in sand. The elevator shot Miss Johnson and the Freeds to the Rainbow Room on the eleventh floor. There they were warmly welcomed.

Rainbow Room! Indeed, at first it was as if they were floating in rainbows. They were dazzled. The contest winners sat at the speakers' table. On Little Joe's right sat the Legion's state commander. On his left sat a state senator. Uniforms! Honorables! The plates were served. But all of the delicious food tasted alike to Little Joe. It could have been library paste stirred together. The other Freeds sat not far away with Miss Johnson, at one of the many small tables. Every time Little Joe looked at Mommy, she was smiling at him. She was all dark lustre and shine. On her shoulder was pinned a beautiful corsage, the same as had been presented to the mothers of the other contest winners.

At last the dessert was served. Cherry pie, but it seemed like more library paste to Little Joe. The commander stood up. He made a fine little speech. He introduced the winner of the first prize. She was a tall, serious eighth-grader from the northern section of the state. She read her essay. Little Joe listened intently. It was different from his composition. It was much more grown-up and learned. He knew, clearly, that it was very good. The judges had been right, thought Little Joe, in awarding the eighth-grader first prize. He applauded her, warmly.

Now it was Little Joe's turn. He stood up, feeling extremely small and skinny. His voice seemed at first to be no louder than the squeak of a mouse. But Mommy and Abraham Lincoln soon put Little Joe at his ease. He read his paper well. The claping was long and loud. Several handkerchiefs in the room were dampened. Dear Miss Johnson's nose, which was of a kind to redden and swell when she shed even the smallest tear, looked as if a hornet had stung it. Mommy didn't cry. She just shone! Poppy was the biggest man in the room, at least in size. India Rose and Pearlie May sparkled like morning stars at their brightest.

The winner of the third prize was a seventh-grader from an adjoining county. The audience in the Rainbow Room did not listen to her as much as they looked at her. For she was extremely pretty, and flashed dazzling rainbow smiles at everyone all the time she read her essay.

The state senator now made a speech. It was a lot of tiresome twaddle. Everyone listening decided not to vote for him at the next election.

But at last the commander stood up again, and presented the awards. He couldn't actually hand to the first prize-winner the flyer to Washington, plus a hotel room and sight-seeing tickets. But the winner knew, and everyone knew, that by this time next week she would be gallivanting around in the nation's capital.

The crisp new bills, fifty dollars worth, which the commander next presented to Little Joe, had never been used by anyone. Little Joe stood up, and said, as Miss Johnson had advised, "Thank you very much, Commander. I am very happy." Happy? *Boy,* that wasn't half of it!

All at once the commander's uniform seemed rather too tight across the chest. It did not take much guessing to see that he was bursting with a wonderful secret. Pretending to be very serious, he said to Little Joe, but loud enough for everyone to hear, "You had better hold onto the table, Joseph, because I have a fine surprise for you." Then, turning to the audience, the commander announced, "A certain neighbor of Joseph's is at present recovering from injuries in the Good Samaritan Hospital here in Rozella. I am happy to tell you that within the last half hour he has sent, by special messenger, twenty-five dollars to add to Joseph's prize money. The neighbor is Mr. Mort Carle."

Glory to goodness! "Doodah, doodah!" Little Joe's eyes fairly popped. Then that old grin of his, catching as measles, wider and happier than ever, spread over his face. How the people laughed and clapped, rejoicing for Joseph Booker Freed!

So then the third prize was awarded, and the bewitching little girl smiled as prettily as if she had won all three prizes. The party broke up, with much talk and hand-shaking. The whole affair had been simply star-spangled!

Going home, Miss Johnson rather recklessly exceeded the speed limit. Everyone was in a gay mood, making silly jokes and laughing uproariously. Poppy slid his hand into Little Joe's pocket, pretending to rob him of his prize money. The boy felt like a millionaire, peeling bills from the fat roll, repaying Poppy for the funds he had needed to buy his new clothes.

"I'm hungry," declared Little Joe. Surely he had eaten nothing since yesterday, except library paste! At the word "hungry," his sisters began giggling at a great rate. And they almost bounced through the top of the car when Little Joe announced grandly that he would treat everyone to ice cream.

Miss Johnson stopped at a crossroads store not far from the farm. Little Joe bought two quarts of cream. When they reached home, Miss Johnson was implored to come in and help eat the ice cream. "I'd love to," she answered. "But I'm setting out for the Lakes at five o'clock tomorrow morning, and I haven't done my packing." She drove off gaily, followed by the Freeds' farewell thanks and good wishes.

In the house, Poppy started to take off his coat and make himself comfortable. But Mommy said, "Keep it on a mite longer, Big Joe, in honor of the day."

Poppy grinned and shrugged his coat on again. "This day!" he exclaimed. "Things have turned out in real Lady Cake style for the Freeds!"

India Rose and Pearlie May almost went into conniptions. While Mommy carried in heaping bowls of ice cream, the sisters tickle-toed to the kitchen. They tickle-toed back, carrying between them a huge round cake. It was mountain-high with frosting.

"This is *Lady Cake,* Little Joe!" they cried. "Poppy, this is real-for-sure Lady Cake. Mommy made it. We whipped the eggs. It took ten egg-whites to make this Lady Cake."

Then the girls ran to the cellar. They flew up again, as if on wings, carrying four wreaths, made

HOW TO MAKE A LIVING ON THE SMALL FARM.

from clover heads, and flowers from Mommy's garden. Even Mommy didn't know the girls had made the wreaths. One was placed around the cake. One went around the dictionary. One was hung over Abraham Lincoln. The prettiest wreath crowned Mommy's head.

"A wreath for a lady," said Poppy, making Mommy a bow. "I think, children," Poppy went on, "that maybe the reason everything has turned out to be Lady Cake for us is because of Mommy."

"Poppy!" cried India Rose, sparkling with a sudden bright idea. "Why don't we call our place *Ladycake Farm?* When a thing is very nice, you're always saying it's 'Lady Cake.' And our farm is nice —the very nicest thing that ever happened to us!"

"Oh, yes, that's what we must call it!" sang Pearlie May. "Because our mommy is a lady, and has baked us a real-for-sure Lady Cake!"

"*Ladycake!* That is exactly the right name!" cried Little Joe.

So that's how it happened that Pearlie May, India Rose, and Little Joe Freed named their new home,

LADYCAKE FARM

The End